# Through The Gate

RACHEL ROY

Cover Art by Ryan Meashaw

# Contents

Author's note:                                    139

# Prologue

S he walked through the gate and up the long drive, casting the events of the day through her mind. She stopped walking before she realized why. She had just rounded the last bend when she had stopped, and now her eyes darted over the several black suv's and limo in her drive. More than that, her attention was on the men in uniform standing around the vehicles. One uniformed man was just stepping out of the house, slamming the door behind himself.

"I see you, Alder." The soft, gravelly voice stopped her in her tracks before Joneya slipped back behind the bend, back to safety. Damn. That greeting gave so much information at once. Her eyes snapped shut so her brain could process faster, she cart wheeled through time to her childhood and back again. Sir Ned would come out of the shadows and softly say 'I see you' when he had to pull her back to duties. It was their code to know that even while she successfully hid from everyone else, that he, her guardian, could find her, and now it was time to return. Now he said those words again. After a decade, she had hoped this time her hiding spot might last.

Rough hands grabbed Joneya. "I got her!" yelled a voice. The hands jerked her arms forward, but she held her feet rooted still.

"Release. Her. Now." That soft, gravelly voice could also be hard and cold, seemingly booming loud even though it was almost a whisper. The hands immediately released, and she felt the men step back.

Alder. That simple nickname held so much information, too. First, he wasn't using her given name, that was for her safety. It was one of many call signs used for her when her name couldn't be spoken over radio communication, but this one he used to her face when he needed her to know that the formality was much, much more than politics and royalty. It was about something older and deeper and of The Family. Alder was her druidic sign, but almost no one knew that true birthdays were kept secret. The wind might blow as it may, but we must bend before the wind to be strong.

Joneya opened her eyes, "The wind blows as it may. I see thee, Sir Hand." His eyes barely lowered in a nod and his smile almost showed before Sir Ned was stone faced again. They stared at each other for a moment. He had more gray and wrinkles and yet seemed hardly changed. She, on the other hand, had grown up from the twenty-something runaway to the thirty-something woman standing before him. So much like her mother. Their eyes locked for a moment. Then she glanced to the house, he nodded, so she walked in as he followed. So did three other men in uniform.

"I'm sorry, my Lady." Her eyebrows moved at the change of address. Again, four words with so much information. Apparently, the queen was dead, which meant what, exactly? The daughter heir had died years ago in a tragic accident, which left whom in the royal line? Oh, the feuding would be epic! But clearly the news hadn't hit the AP wire yet, or she would have seen and heard already.

Her eyes flicked over the men; she didn't know the three who had followed them in. "I did not expect this news today." No tears for the woman who had always been a room away. Or more often, an entire neighborhood away. Sir Ned and his wife had cleaned up more of her scraped knees than the woman with the beautiful long hair, pristine gowns, and the diamond crown. She had nothing in common with that woman. Well, very little.

Sir Ned, also known by his title, The Hand of the King. Except truly, his title was Angbor D'elyar - Fist of the Blood. Most people assumed Blood meant the royal bloodline and so the title had changed in the common tongue. Some remembered that the powerful families of old were not always those of the royal lineage. Though to be fair, often the royal lineage was based upon the ones who held the power. Quite a few believed the power, then and now, was of the old ways. Few claimed to be a druid now, but every child of the "powerful" families played a game when they were young. That game had them guessing the secret code by looking at symbols and lines. If they decoded the first secrets on paper, they then moved to the second level and tried to read the secrets on the rock. Very few children could ever read the secrets, and those who did kept the secrets safe. Sir Ned played the game with Joneya. The secrets had inevitably led her to this day.

"Sir Ned, my children will be home soon." She stated this not as a question nor as an imperative, but to state the information, to formulate a plan forward.

"Yes." Sir Ned nodded. "Would you care for assistance packing a bag for the next day?"

"Only for a day?" She arched an eyebrow slightly.

"You only need to pack for a day, my Lady." Was there a slight emphasis on packing? His answer was clarified when Sir Ned continued,

"The men will close up the house, and two men will stay here. As to your dog,..."

Joneya did smile internally then, picturing the men as they tried to command the 140 pound Rottweiler to do anything that he didn't want to. Most likely, he had allowed them into her room and then had them frozen in place, terrified to move another inch or be eviscerated. "My puppy will come with me."

"Yes. Of course. Could you perhaps convince your, um, puppy to allow the men to breathe again?" She could hear the smile he was holding back.

"I could. But, I may not. They have no business in my room."

"Lady, we were just-"began one of the men in uniform.

"Silence." Joneya and Sir Ned said in unison. She continued on, "I am not happy that you are here, in my home. I understand you are here by orders, not by choice. I, however, am a bitch by choice and family curse. I will not tolerate certain things and an invasion into my, or my children's space, is one of those things I will not tolerate. In the future, you would all do well to stay out of my personal quarters unless invited. Nor, for the record, do I tolerate lying, thieving, or hypocrisy. If you intend to stay in my employ, or my proximity, I expect respect." Softer she continued, "In return, I will respect you. If you do not follow this simple philosophy, I will make your life a living hell. You should explain this to your friends. And perhaps your enemies as well."

"Yes, Ma'am." The poor man-boy looked like he might swallow his tongue and certainly wished he might escape immediately.

"My Lady, the men, your dog. Please." Sir Ned was indeed still a man of few words, as if secrets might spill if he used too many words.

She met his eyes, frowned, and acquiesced. At Joneya's first whistle, she knew his ears perked forward. With her second whistle, he stood up. The five of them could hear his nails on the floorboards above.

At her third whistle, a different note combination, the puppy came tearing down the stairs, bounding across the room, and sat at attention by her hand. She laid her hand on his head and rubbed behind his ears. "Good boy, Sere*." She raised an eyebrow at the three man-boys. They shuffled their feet and avoided her eyes. Except one, the one she had just chewed out.

He grinned. "Nice, my Lady. Very nice." She smiled then; he had potential.

*Sere - peace.

# Chapter 1 - Changes

The two children boarded the plane beside her. The dog, Sere, followed so closely that he kept stepping on their heels despite their scolding. While the children were a little nervous, quite excited, and a bit confused, Joneya was not particularly nervous (not at all for the plane ride), and was considering a tattoo of a strong, bending tree. We must bow before the wind if we wish to weather the storm. This would be the storm of the century.

They boarded the private jet, led and followed by uniformed men. "Mom," the seventeen-year-old boy with piercing blue eyes asked, "how long is this flight?"

"I'm not sure exactly." She replied. "We'll have plenty of time to get settled, eat supper, watch a movie or read, and then go to sleep. Sleeping may be hard, but tomorrow is going to be very busy and it will be tomorrow when we land."

"Wait!" said the blond-haired girl with the long ponytail. "We're eating supper on the plane?"

"Yes," smiled the woman. "Or else we'll be really hungry. We can't land on the ocean, get out and eat." She could see Sir Ned biting his cheek to keep from laughing. The blond-haired girl rolled her eyes. "Obvs. What are we eating?"

"I don't know. But I'm sure they have planned ahead to accommodate what we like." Joneya knew it was a little overwhelming to be basically ripped out of your home after school. It would only get worse. She could explain everything in detail or she could be nonchalant about some of it. There were no parenting handbooks that covered this, and her own mother hadn't prepared her at all.

"But they're definitely meeting us here?" asked Elfrya, her ponytail swung as she peered around.

Sir Ned cut in, "I assure you, child, we will not leave without the rest of your family." And just like that, the concerns that Joneya had about her blended family being pushed apart evaporated like a popping soap bubble.

Then, a loud, familiar 12-year-old's voice could be heard, "This is dope. How long is this tunnel? In the movies, they're really short. Is this what you go on all the time, Arigail?"

"I'd say they're here," said Larseth dryly.

As Larseth spoke, Joneya's husband, Abaris, stepped onto the plane followed by his son and daughter. His eyes immediately found hers, and she smiled in welcome. "You ok?"

"Yeah." There really weren't words to explain all the emotions raging through her. She pushed them all aside to rage like winds in a storm, set her roots deep, and went with the flow. "I'd like you to meet Sir Ned. The most honorable man I know."

As soon as Abaris saw she was ok, the tension went out of his shoulders. The men shook hands, judging each other, and a little surprised at each other's strength of character. Ever the impatient one,

Arigail grabbed Ravous' hand and darted over to Elfrya. The four kids wandered forward in the plane, which was nothing like any of them had been on.

Ravenous' voice floated back, "It's like Air Force One, this plane."

"We'll be taking off directly, m'lady," said Sir Ned. "Make yourselves comfortable."

Indeed, the plane was like the presidential airplane. It had some rows of seats, but it also had a section more like a den or study, a boardroom, and a game room (where the kids were). Then small sleeping quarters. A couple of small bathrooms and a galley completed the spaces. The pilot and front of the plane were curtained off, although there was a door that could be pulled shut. There were actually emergency doors through the plane that were bulletproof and could section off the plane should the need arise, but it was designed to appear as open as possible.

Joneya and Abaris settled into the study after looking in on the kids. Staff were delivering them sodas, and some snacks were in the center of the room. As soon as Abaris had settled, a cold beer and a shaker of salt were set near him. A glass of red wine was handed to Joneya.

"You don't have to be the hidden sister." Sir Ned was always bluntly honest. "But whatever you choose must be decided on this flight. Once we step off, there is no changing your mind. Your family doesn't get to change their minds."

"Family, Sir Ned?"

"Aye, Lass. Your family." He smiled at her fondly. "The ones who raised you and the ones you raise."

She tipped her head back against the back of the couch and rubbed her temple with her right hand. Abaris slipped his strong hand under her hair and pushed her head forward. Then he rubbed some of the tension out of her neck. Had they been alone, he would have taken off her shirt and had her lay face down with her head in his lap so he could rub her neck and shoulders better. But that didn't seem appropriate with Sir Ned there, even though it was completely non-sexual.

"Yeah, I need a plan." As usual, Sir Ned said nothing. He let her mind whirl. They both knew the ramifications of her choice. It wasn't just her affected, nor her and her family, but everyone in her lands. No matter what her choice, it would always be her lands, it was her role that she had some choice in.

"I'll leave you be, Lass. Let me or one of the boys know if you need something." Sir Ned slipped out of the room, leaving Abaris and Joneya their first real chance to talk since this whirlwind started hours ago.

"Are you going to tell me, just What. The. Fuck. is going on now?" asked Abaris. Actually, Joneya was surprised he had held it together this long. He wasn't loud or angry, but he was tense. Tense was an understatement, she was sure. He had just had the rug, and the floor, and the foundation swept out from under him and his kids. He knew a little about her childhood, but not enough to understand all this. He trusted her, or he never would have gotten on the plane.

"Yeah. Short version first?" He nodded, and she continued. "My mother, the Royal Queen Lady, preferred her second daughter over me. When I was little, I didn't understand why and so I hid a lot. Later, I came to understand. But regardless, I hid by myself a lot, but Sir Ned, The Fist of the Blood, or Hand of the King-"

"Like Game of Thrones ®?"

"Uhh, yeah, kinda. Anyway, he always knew where I was, even when I thought I was hidden away. Eventually, he and his wife basically adopted me. It didn't take long before the people kind of forgot that there had been two of us girls. We're very different. We both had the lessons in leadership and politics, but then we differed. She learned more about hosting dignitaries, and I learned more about history. She's smart, but we had very different educations. She's the front page princess and I'm the one behind the veil. I am the eldest though, so if I want my mother's crown, it can be mine."

"What?!"

"Yeah." She made a face. "Technically, I'm the queen right now and my sister is the queen regent. However, I'm sure she intends to be queen. That is what she was raised to be."

"Seriously?"

"Yeah. Have another beer. You may need it." She rubbed her forehead some more. "There are two levels of reign though. One is a bit, well no, it's almost completely secret. I have that and always will. The question is whether I want the royal throne to go with it."

"This is your hippy, witchyness, isn't it?"

Joneya barked out a laugh. "Yeah, simplistically it's my hippy, witchyness." She looked him full in the eyes. "I don't want the throne or those politics. But if you want me to consider it more, I will."

"Baby, I want you to do what makes you happy. But I am not dealing with pretentious people every day and changing who I am to be more 'appropriate'." He paused and then smirked. "I do look good dressed up, though."

"Oh, you can still dress up. And we'll still be involved in court, but far less than some might want." She laughed then, and overtired, verging towards hysterical sounding, but truly honest, laughter. "And almost no one can tell me what or when to do anything."

"I don't think that's how it works."

"Oh no," she chuckled, "that's exactly how it works when you can claim High Queen Priestess for your title." She grabbed her glass of wine and swallowed it down. "Because that's the blood that I have and she doesn't. Daddy dear isn't actually my daddy, and mother hates it.

Hated it. But I have what my sister doesn't, and push comes to shove, I'm the one with the real strength."

# Chapter 2 - Coming Home

Immediately upon landing at the airport, they were met by black, official looking cars with tinted (and bulletproof) glass. The kids were amazed; the dog didn't care, and Abaris handled it with style. Joneya really didn't notice the ride at all until they were almost to the destination.

"Stop, Driver," she ordered.

He looked back in the mirror and raised his eyebrows in question.

"It's not an emergency, but pull over." She clarified. He immediately adjusted and pulled to the side of the road. Sir Ned slid over and held the door for her as she said, "You guys can stay here, but I need a moment." She paused a moment more. "Or you can get out and stretch if you want, but don't talk to anyone who didn't come with us. And if you see a single reporter, you get your butts back in the car." She made eye contact with the driver and he gave a slight nod. He'd watch for strangers, as would the rest of the escort ahead and behind them. She was sure they were on satellite cameras being watched too, and her sister fuming that they had stopped. But she could deal.

"Do you want to go alone?" asked Sir Ned. They both knew by alone he really meant, "Do you want the escort to fan out and stay out of your sight, or can a couple of us walk beside you?"

"I don't need to be alone." He gave some orders, and they began walking to the enormous tree in the center of the park. The grass was cared for, but not trampled, like it was important but not used. The further they walked in, the more it felt like sacred ground. Like the graveyard behind a church that is centuries old, or the ruins of ancient civilizations. There's a hush and a heaviness in the air, and one tends to speak softly.

Joneya walked directly to the tree and leaned both palms against it. Her eyes closed, and she focussed completely on the feel of the rough bark beneath her hands. The wind gusted for a moment and blew her hair, billowing the dress she was wearing. Joneya let her awareness spread through the trunk and then the whispering leaves above. She could feel the strength of the tree with roots deep in the earth, powerful energy held within. She took deep breaths, smelling the dirt and the wood, and the air. The breeze teased her face again, pushing her hair out of her face and whispering secrets with just a hint of the sea swirled after by fresh grass. Sun broke through the clouds and a shaft of sunlight snuck through the branches to warm her back. The tree, the roots, the earth, her body, her hands to the trunk made a circle of energy. She felt the earth through her feet just as easily as she felt the tree through her hands. It would have been stronger if she were barefoot like normal; still she could feel the hum of earth and life circling through her, the tree, and the ground. Her shoulders relaxed. She tipped her head back and felt the sunlight upon her eyelids and her cheeks. A few more deep breaths, pushing her energy into the circle and pulling cleansing strength in. She caressed the tree and stepped back.

"Ready, Lass?"

"Yes." She opened her eyes and looked directly into his blue eyes. "Let's do this."

They walked back to the car. One of the escort men had already opened the door and started ushering her family back in as soon as she and Sir Ned had turned back to the car. As soon as the car door shut, the driver pulled out. "Trouble?" asked Sir Ned.

"Cars approaching with untraceable tags," the driver quietly responded.

Characteristically, Sir Ned didn't reply.

Ravous asked what the other kids were wondering, "What does that mean? Unknown tags?"

"It means that there are vehicles coming with plates that can't be tracked," answered Joneya. "That means that there is a reason they can't be tracked. Either they're government or they're fake. Either way, since we're not expecting them, we're leaving."

"Why? Are they dangerous?"

"We don't know who they are, so we don't know if they are dangerous." Joneya made eye contact with Abaris. "Here's the deal. Everything changes today - it already has. Think of every movie you have seen with the president and his family, or diplomats and their families, or royal families. You each have a guard assigned to you at all times. You'll help me choose who your regular day-to-day person is later. And we always have a group of people watching us. All the time."

"Like the Secret Service?"

"Uhhuh." Joneya didn't bother adding that not only was it the "good guys" who would keep track of them.

Abaris noticed that two more of their cars pulled in around the car that they were riding in, but he didn't say anything either. There weren't any incidents, and they soon arrived at tall gates in a high stone wall. They were expected, and the gates began to swing out even as they pulled in close. Guards stood at attention on both sides of the gate. They didn't block them, but they didn't greet them either. Their car rolled through, with two others flanking them, and they drove up a long drive.

"Where are we?" asked the girls almost simultaneously.

The door by Abaris opened, and the footman said, "Welcome to Castle Draug."

"Castle Dog?!" asked Ravous with glee.

Joneya snorted. "Close. Draug, not dog. Castle Draug."

"Oh." Ravous was disappointed

"But," said Sir Ned, familiar with young boys, "it means Castle Wolf."

"Oh cool! Hey Mom, that's your favorite animal!"

"Uhhuh."

"Wait," asked Larseth, speaking for the first time in a while. "Have you been here before, Mom."

"Yeah. This-" she took a deep breath, "This is where I grew up before I went to live with my aunt and uncle."

"You lived in a castle?!"

"Uhhuh. But it wasn't as fun as it sounds. Nothing like the movies. C'mon." The footman was still standing at attention by the car door and they all slid out.

"I've been directed to tell you, Sir Hand, that you will meet in the King's quarters. The living room." The footman lowered his eyes. "You are directed to go there first."

Sir Ned raised an eyebrow, and the poor footman blushed. "I'm sor-"

"You did well following directions, lad. Say no more," interrupted Sir Ned. The footman ducked his head, cheeks aflame.

Mentally, Joneya pushed her feet, her soul, down into the ground and pulled up a pillar of strength and protection to envelop her and her family. She let her shoulders down and strode forward. As soon as she reached the door, it swung in on silent hinges. She barely hesitated as she stepped over the threshold and saw nearly every castle employee lined up in the hall. Men and women in castle uniforms stood at each side. Her eyes filled with tears and she bit the inside of her lip. Instead of striding forward at her normal pace, she stepped to the side and grabbed Abaris' hand and pulled him beside her. He caught on immediately and gathered the children in next. Joneya smiled, trying to connect with everyone standing and waiting for her.

"Thank you," she paused. They all knew the politics, the game of thrones or the game of power or whatever you wanted to name it. They were not instructed to wait and greet her. They had chosen to. Many of them remembered the little girl who had hid all through the castle, and often sprung up to lend a helping hand, or with childish chatter who had grown into a pleasant young woman before just leaving one day. This was a solid show of support for her. Not her family, not her roles, but for her. "I want to introduce you to my family." One by one, she named them each, and the staff bowed to each of them. For once, her children were polite and subdued.

"Welcome home, M'Lady," said several of the older adults as they walked down the hall. She reached the end of the welcome committee and turned back. "I'm not sure where exactly we'll be residing, but I appreciate this welcome more than you know. I'll see you all later."

Joneya purposely slowed her pace to let her family look around a little as they traveled through a maze of hallways, headed to the King's Apartments. An interesting place to meet. Informal and intimate, but neutral, unlike the royal audience rooms or the Queen's Apartments.

She nodded to the guards as they came up to heavy, gold doors with purple inlaid between dark mahogany wood. She snapped her fingers and Sere stood with his ears brushing her hand. The doors opened and she, Abaris, and Sere stepped through, followed by more hesitant children.

There were only a few people in the room. Abaris hesitated for just a moment and then followed Joneya in farther. He was shocked to see a woman who could be her twin, sitting in a dark purple over-chair.

"Shit, she looks just like Mom," whispered one of the children. It was a very loud whisper for such a silent room.

Joneya hesitated just a moment and then smiled. "Kids come meet your aunt, Her Royal Highness, Queen Francesca of House Draug." At those words, at that title, Francesca visibly relaxed and smiled.

"Hello everyone, come on in. I won't bite. We'll have some food brought in for you. If you're like my kids, you're always hungry."

Thinking it would all be fancy food like froi gois and sushi, the children politely declined. Francesca looked surprised, but quickly understood and laughed. "It's not like the movies. We have 'normal' food and soda."

\*\*\*

Quickly, life outside Castle Draug became quite normal. There was room at the castle for Joneya, Abaris, and their family, but they quickly agreed that castle life, and never any alone time, was not for them. They spent two days there, letting the cousins get to know each other, and attending many boring state functions surrounding the death of the ruling monarch. Joneya was able to stay away from speeches and toasts, but more and more her name was included, as if she had never left.

But unlike her sister's quarters, Joneya and her family always had little extras. The staff quickly learned preferred treats and vices (chewing tobacco was not common in the area and especially not the particular brand of Wintergreen, Fine Cut) and these were always available in their apartments. By the second day, gifts began arriving from outside the castle. Fresh baked bread in a gorgeous basket, a beautifully woven shawl, an intricately modeled boat, and even a live goose - that did not stay in the apartment.

On the third day, they moved to House Isilme. A sprawling grey stone building with matching outbuildings and barns, gardens, orchards, and surrounded by a stone wall that formed a perfect circle despite the knolls and streams.

"Mom," asked Larseth, "What does I-seel-may mean?"

"Isilme," Joneya smiled. "Swallow the middle more. House of Moonlight."

"Mmm. Is it because of the gray color? So it looks the same day or night."

"Hmm?" She pondered this. It wasn't really that simple, but when delved into the heart of the matter, it kinda was. "Maybe. I'm not sure. It's ancient, so I'm not sure that anyone knows."

The kids quickly had their Wi-Fi connections, tvs, bikes, dirt bikes, and even horses available. There were always dogs and cats about, along with pastures of other animals. Sere was usually right at Joneya's side, but she did enjoy frolicking with the other dogs. The first night, Abaris found that there was a barroom set up like a sports bar with the big screen tvs but it also had a poker table set off to the side. Joneya had a library of her own with a heavy table in front of a huge shelf of maps, and a lighter table set up by the windows, comfy chairs and sofas, and so many books. Plants were placed strategically throughout the room, and the Wi-Fi signal was excellent. Special glass that could only be seen through at a direct angle showed her the views from all the security cameras of House Isilme when she sat behind the desk. Stepping directly outside onto a veranda let her step directly into the greenhouse within about two paces. Heat and moisture tend to be bad for books and maps, otherwise the two rooms would have been directly connected.

Soon visitors began to arrive. The gifts continued to arrive, and Joneya soon had a system for the gifts to be redistributed to those more in need of it, but recorded so that she could thank each giver. Some gifts were a welcome home. A few were reminders of shared pasts. Some were to curry favor. A few carried messages in their depths. As common as the gifts were the visitors who wanted to speak with "The Lady".

"Who is 'The Lady'?" asked Arigail one day at breakfast. Joneya wasn't there, but when she wasn't, she always arranged for Mariella or one of the other friendly house servants to be present.

"There are many ladies of our history, my dear," answered Mariella. "But I think you have heard it recently here. The title is actually Lady of the Moonlight."

"Oh. What's that?" continued Arigail.

"Why, it's your mother, dear," gently laughed Mariella. "She's the one that so many come to for answers or help."

"Help? How does she help?" asked Elfrya.

"Hmm," there was a lot that Mariella didn't think the children knew. "She knows many people, and she knows the lands well, so she can often make arrangements for people who need help, or find special ways for people to work together." The children absorbed this answer. "Now finish up," Mariella changed the subject, "you have a busy day exploring the property, remember?"

"Oh, that's right!" exclaimed Ravous, "I forgot we are going on a four wheeler adventure today. That Ben guy is going to show us around, right?"

"I think it's Ben, yes," answered Mariella. "Remind me though, what's the one area you DO NOT go?"

"By the Murky Pond," all four kids answered.

"Mom said there's sink holes and stuff, so it's too dangerous," added Ravous.

"Yes, it is dangerous and many people have drowned there." Mariella agreed with him, but held back her further knowledge. "I don't go there either. Almost no one does, only a couple seem to know where to step safely." Whew, tricky stepping there. Not so much the land itself that was dangerous, but there were some sinkholes. If they believe the sinkholes lead to the many drownings, so be it.

A line of petitioners for time with Joneya had already formed. There were young and old, men and women, but it was the style of dress that varied the most. There were some dressed in scruffy jeans and t-shirts, some in formal business attire, and not a few in fancy robes. One young lady was even dressed all in leather. Joneya saw them in the order they arrived except for the young woman with the baby. All the petitioners agreed to let them ahead in the queue before the baby woke up and fussed.

"M'Lady," the young maid from Castle Draug spoke softly. "I have been sent to see if you will permanently reside here, or if you'll be coming back to your royal apartments."

"No, Emily," the servant started with the use of her name. "I don't intend to spend any more nights under that roof. Why do you ask?"

"I, well, that is-"

"It's alright Emily, you're safe here."

"Yes, mum," Emily took a deep breath and pulled herself up. She was, after all, a royal servant and knew how to carry herself, emotions buried. "Yes, mum, there was just a bit of a question as a number of people would like to speak with you, but traveling can be mighty difficult for some people."

"Hmm, I see." Joneya pondered for a moment. "This is the message you bring back to whomever needs to hear it." The maid nodded that she was listening. "You tell anyone who needs to speak with me that they may come any time. If they cannot come here, for whatever reason, then they may pass or send any note or letter to me."

"But-"

Joneya held up one finger to pause the maid, "But if they do not want anything written, and for that matter they may email too, but if they don't want it written, then they may have one of you, a trusted friend, bring their request to me and I'll do my best to help, just as if they were standing in front of me."

The maid nodded. "Thank you, mum."

"Will that work, do you think?"

"I think it will, mum."

"In fact," Joneya chewed her bottom lip, thinking. "I think there may be some books that I would like to borrow from Castle Draug's library. Certainly, I may need books carried back and forth weekly. I wonder if there might be a castle servant, one such as yourself perhaps, who might transport those for me?"

"Oh yes, Mum," the maid smiled widely, looking relieved. "I am quite sure one of us could help you that way."

"Good. Head off then, and I'll see what I can do for your niece as you asked, alright?'

"Yes mum. You have a good day, mum."

After the maid was a woman from the local village. She brought concerns about the taxes that had been levied previously paid to Castle Draug, but with concerns now that the House Isilme was also occupied. Joneya made note to look into the taxes and which entity had the responsibilities for roads and such.

Soon after, two old men came in to ask about their distillery rights. She promised them that the Lord Abaris would come by to see their operation. She suggested that they might have small samples for him.

Next in the queue was a man of undetermined age who quite seemed to be homeless. Shortly after he sat down, a number of waiting patrons left while covering their mouths and noses. Then he began to cough and hack; every other person in her waiting room suddenly remembered somewhere else to be.

The butler knocked and came into the library. Joneya raised an eyebrow. "Well, send the next one. The sooner I see them, perhaps the sooner I'll be done for the day."

The butler looked uncomfortable and said, "M'lady, there is only one more left, but I don't think you want to see him."

Her eyebrows shot up. "No?" she asked, "Why not?"

"Well, umm mum, he," the poor butler turned bright red as he stumbled over his words. "He, um, is quite dirty, mum."

"A little dirt is fine."

"Ah, no mum. I mean he's very dirty," the poor butler looked very uncomfortable. He leaned forward and whispered, "He's a lot dirty and he smells terrible."

"I see." Joneya wasn't thrilled, but she wasn't going to turn someone away because he seemed homeless. "Bring him out to the veranda."

"Umm, yes, mum."

The butler immediately returned with the dirty man, and simultaneously the wind shifted, carrying his stench directly to Joneya. She didn't bat an eye, although her breath hitched. The butler had been caught by the shifting wind as well and tried very hard not to gag, although his face turned deathly pale.

"Thank you, Jeeves," said Joneya, giving leave to the butler, who did his best to leave with a stately run.

As soon as he was out of sight, the man tore off the nasty jacket he was wearing and the baseball hat. He tossed them far out on the grass and downwind. "Thank the gods! I thought you would never get to me, and that stench was making my eyes water."

Actually seeing his face, Joneya just started laughing. "Seriously?" she grinned. "You couldn't just say hello like a normal person, Cuz?"

"And let everyone, including her royal-stick-up-her-ass-perfect-photo, know I was here? Certainly not."

"Hmm. Sit down, but first help me grab something to drink. I have a mini fridge in here." Joneya stepped back into the library, motioning him in.

"Do you have any snacks there, too? I seemed to have missed a meal or three traveling here."

"Umm, yeah, I have cookies and uh, yogurt maybe...I don't know, take a look."

***

Later, she was having tea on the veranda with Abaris. A young man was shown out to them. "I'm sorry to bother you, M'Lady," he said, ducking his head.

"No worries. What do you need?" He seemed slightly taken aback by such informality.

"I uh, yeah. I have applied to Grecquao University."

"Really?" asked Joneya, fully aware of how esteemed that university was. "Have you been accepted?"

"Yes, mum." he grinned with pride. "That's why I'm here, mum. I need a royal approval to attend."

"The queen won't agree to that?" Joneya's eyebrows jumped in surprise.

"No, that is, I'm not sure," the young man now stumbled over his words. "I haven't asked her, mum. I wanted your permission, mum."

"Hmm." Joneya pondered the implications of this. "I-"

He quickly interrupted her, "I know you appreciate the learning more, mum. It would mean something to my heart if you would sign off."

"Mmmmhmm." Joneya pursed her lips a moment, eyeing him. "First, congratulations. You had to earn that acceptance." The young man ducked his head in thanks. "Second, because of that, I know you're smart enough to understand my next point. I need to consider if there are wider repercussions of my granting this. I'm confident you will be granted leave, but I'm not sure it's my place to do so. At least politically..." Sensing more, she asked him, "Is there something else you need?"

He sighed a little in relief, probably unsure of how he would have broached the next piece. "It's me Grandmum." He said in a rush. "She's a bit old, and maybe showing signs that she'll be slightly daft in a few years. I'm worried about her."

"Is someone threatening her?" Joneya leaned forward.

"Oh no, mum, not that." I mean, I'm worried that something may run amiss while I'm gone. You see now I'm in a flat just down the street from her and I can check in daily, but when I'm gone...well, I have friends who can check in some, but it won't be every day like."

"I see." Joneya appreciated his concern for his grandmother. "Would you want her to move in here, in my house, while you are gone?"

"Oh no, mum. I couldn't so impose." he laughed bitterly, "Nor would she accept that. She's fiercely independent, worse since her daughter, me mum, was killed in a car accident." Joneya murmured condolences, but the young man just kept speaking. "No, I was hoping that you might have a task that she could do for the house, some work that might require someone to fetch her or her work every few days. Then, if I know you had someone able to check on her as well as me cousins and friends, there could be someone checking on her every day. Plus, she would feel useful, like, if she were working for you. It would keep her organized, I think."

"Mhhhm. We can arrange something like that. You go home then, see if you can work around a conversation to see if there is something that she would particularly enjoy doing, whether it's cooking a particular sweet roll, or teaching someone a skill. See what she enjoys and I'll figure it out. She might not be connected directly here, though. I might find her skills are needed within the village or something, but it will be someone I trust looking on and checking a couple of times a week. Ok?"

"Oh yes, mum," He sounded so relieved. "No mum, it doesn't have to be here, but something that makes her happy. And, if you're looking after her, I know she'll be ok."

"Good. Go ahead then and send word with what you think she might enjoy most."

"Yes mum. You have a good afternoon, mum." He nearly bowed on his way off the veranda and back the way he'd come.

"Not even tea in peace?" asked Abaris with a chuckle.

Joneya snorted. "We had like ten minutes alone." She smiled slyly then. "I think you should arrange a date in your bar tonight. Just us. If you have anything I like to drink there."

"Oh, I think I can make you something you like to drink."

"Good." They both grinned.

"Hey, I have a question." Abaris said. Joneya nodded with a questioning look. "Why do they call you mom?"

"Mom?" asked Joneya, confused. "Oh. It's the accent. It's not 'mom' it's 'mum'."

"OK," he asked with exaggerated patience, "why do they call you 'mum'?"

"It's a less formal, formal address." Joneya had another sip of her hard cider, stretched her legs out and leaned back in the chair. She closed her eyes and tipped her face to the sun. Abaris was fully in the shade. They were both content. "It's short for 'madam' actually, though no one would use that. More formal is m'lady or M'lady." You could hear the capital letter in the second. "It's acknowledging my role, but showing comfort or familiarity, too. I prefer it, actually. Or, nothing at all." She laughed ruefully. That won't happen.

"Beltane is this weekend. Do you guys remember what that is?" Joneya asked her children at breakfast.

"It's May Day, right?" asked Elfrya.

"What's that?" asked Arigail.

"Maypoles and flower baskets," answered Elfrya.

"We usually have a bonfire, too," said Larseth.

"Yup, all of this," answered Joneya "but there's a bit more too."

"It marks Spring turning to Summer. Beltane is when people celebrate crops being planted and hoping for good harvests. It's also a time of cleansing and getting rid of the old." Joneya was keeping it simple, and really didn't feel like explaining fertility rituals in any depth. She didn't lie to her children, but she didn't always share everything.

"Is that what the party is this weekend?" asked Arigail.

"Uhhuh."

"A party?" asked Ravous, "Here?"

"Some of it is here and some of it is in the Village, right?" asked Abaris.

"Right. So there's a blessing given here, for all our crops to grow well, and the livestock to be healthy, and for prosperity. Then there is a parade from here to the center of the Village to the MayPole."

"Why is it here?" asked Larseth.

"Because your mother is a bigwig," answered Abaris.

"Really?"

"Kinda," said Joneya, her eyes shooting daggers at Abaris, who grinned back. "I'm the country's official priestess, so I offer the blessing."

"You're a priestess?!"

"I am the official priestess." It was true, she was the official priestess. But she was also the real priestess of the realm, too. The power of a millennia ran through her veins and connected her to the land. The kids were right. They had always celebrated Beltane some at home, but they had no idea how much she really did. "There will be tv stations and newspapers here. You don't have to talk to anyone unless you want to, but I suggest that you don't talk to any reporters. They often twist your words about, so it seems like you said something that you never even thought of saying."

"I don't want to be on tv, anyway!"

"Cool, Elfrya, then you don't need to be," answered Joneya with a smile. "I, on the other hand, don't get a choice. But Sir Ned and his people will help keep the reporters away from you. It would make sense to let them take some pictures of you watching bits and pieces of the celebration. Maybe the parade. If you want to, you can be in the parade."

"Do we get to be in a fancy car and throw candy?" asked Ravous. "Or ride in a fire truck?"

"Ummm," Joneya bit back a smile. "No fire trucks, no. No riding at all, in fact, but you could walk and throw out candy if you like."

"Ugh, no. I don't want to walk. What if it's hot out?"

She did laugh then. "You can just watch, that's fine. Or, you can join in, if you want. You just need to let Sir Ned know if you change your minds at all. He'll help you either way, just let him know."

They all nodded their heads. They were used to having to check in with their bodyguards and tell them what their plans were. They had actually adjusted to that really well.

"Ok, so blessings here, then parade to town, then the MayPole and dancing. After that, it's a big party with food and music. You can stay as long as you want, unless a guard you know tells you to leave. If it's not a guard you know, because there will be a lot of people, refuse to leave until Sir Ned himself, or your regular guard tells you. Daddy and I will be there late. You don't have to stay. But even we won't stay until the very end, because it goes all night."

"Oh, and you get to be a little dressed up for it. Flower crowns for the girls, antler crowns for the boys. Sometimes people dress up like nymphs and fairies. It's fun! Ask the other kids what they'll be doing." Joneya had made sure that there were other families living at or near their house, so there were other kids for her children to interact with. First, they needed friends around, but secondly, they could learn the nuances of the culture better through peers of their own age.

They talked a little more, but really, the kids didn't have many more questions. Later though, she had more info for Abaris. "You have a role too, you know," she gave him a wicked smile.

"Shit, what do I have to do?" he asked with mock fear.

"It won't be too bad. You have to flirt and drink a lot."

"Oh no," he tried to keep a straight face.

"Probably quite a few young ladies will try to kiss you. That's up to you. It is a fertility celebration, so there aren't many rules." She laughed outright at his look of genuine surprise at that. "It's like everyone has a Hall Pass that night. More than a pass, everyone who enjoys it is supposed to fuck."

"This must be a dream come true for the teenage boys."

"Pretty much," she smiled more seriously. "There are a lot of moms getting their girls on birth control this month in preparation. Celebrations are all well and good, but unintended pregnancies are not so much fun."

"You will be the official Stag in the ceremonies, but I'll keep your role easy. You may have to do the binding of the handfasting."

"I have to marry people?"

"No, a local druid will cover the oaths, but you might do the actual winding of the cord. There's a special way to wrap the bindings, but it's not hard."

"I don't want to do any ceremonies," he paused, "I do have the presence for it, though."

"Just like rituals at the Elks, yes, you do. We will definitely lead the lovers out into the woods, and we get to play too. In fact, we need to."

"We have to fuck?"

"We don't. But I do. And I would like it to be with you."

He lifted an eyebrow. "Thanks. I think."

She laughed. "It's more fun than a fancy dinner with political dignitaries. Better beer, too."

"Drinking, music, and fucking. They know how to party here."

"Uhhuh. We'll get you to dance around the late night fires. I think you'll enjoy that smoke, too."

"I don't like bonfire smoke."

"This is called Fairy Smoke or Smoke of the Fae. You'll like it."

"I will, huh?"

"Yup. At least I think so. I tend to avoid it, but you'll like it."

"Smoke of the Fae?"

"Uhhuh."

"Groooooovyyyyy," he said with a grin.

# Chapter 3 - Beltane

The afternoon before Beltane, April 30th, Sir Ned and Joneya slipped out of the house by themselves. Joneya carried a picnic basket and a small wrapped gift. Had anyone noticed them leaving, it wouldn't have seemed strange. Joneya often brought items to the local people. However this time, they headed out to the area that was forbidden. Murky Pond was an area of legend. It was said that if you walked alone out there, that you might not come back. Many missing persons had been found dead along the shore. It was odd, no one knew how deep it was, but there was no current. There was a sandy beach with some large boulders further out. It would be the perfect swimming area, if not for the legends and fears. In fact, the waters were not murky at all, just the history of the place was unclear.

Joneya and Sir Ned walked slowly out. Then Sir Ned stopped a little before reaching the beach and let Joneya walk ahead. She scanned the crystal waters, but saw nothing out of the ordinary. She gave a whistle, similar to what she used for Sere. After standing there for a few minutes, apparently waiting, she set the basket on a flat, table-sized rock. She set a wrapped package on top of the basket, and tucked just under the gift was a photo of her four children and Sere. Kneeling, she dipped her hand in the water. She lifted a handful of water to her lips and blew across it, almost like blowing a kiss, and then poured the water back into the pond. She stood, looking out across the still water again. Then, she turned and walked back to Sir Ned.

They resumed their soft conversation, just chatter, and ambled away. Behind them there was a soft splash and then water puddled on the ground by the rock. Wet fingers softly slid aside the gift and picked up the photo. Green eyes followed Joneya until she was out of sight.

\*\*\*

Preparations began long before dawn, with breads and treats being freshly baked, fancy clothes being ironed, flowers and herbs being picked. Feet danced through the dew, and many maidens washed in cold pools along the streams. Not a few boys tried to sneak into the woods to see those young ladies, but there seemed to be quite a number of women out foraging in those same woods quite early that morning. Joneya and others who worked magic were greeting the rising sun, dancing in the dew, and collecting dew drops in fancy glass vials to then have the first rays of dawn shine through. No predators seemed to be about, and even the most timid animals and birds of the woods seemed to be strutting and singing.

Just before the blessings, the girls were given silver worked flower crowns and ribbons for their hair. The boys received copper antler crowns and silver cuffs for their wrists. Abaris had a spectacular crown of copper leaves and branches that became antlers. Joneya handed him a leather vest to wear over a green polo shirt.

Joneya's outfit was the most ornate. She wore a blue dress for water, a flowing white cloak of fine cashmere for air, flowers woven in her hair and embroidered everywhere for earth, with a crown of fire (rubies and other gems in bronze and copper). She also wore silver bracelets from her wrists, twining up arms and across her back and shoulders, which held her cloak but also matched the crown in design.

With Sir Ned, his wife, and their daughter, Mariella, watching over the children, Abaris joined Joneya in front of the crowd. Before the actual blessing, Joneya reminded the people of the purposes of the rituals. She reminded them that spreading flowers and green boughs is to spread the fertility and growth of harvests. She reminded them that dancing around the bonfires should scare off the troublesome spirits, and spreading those ashes on the pastures protects the livestock from diseases. With a little humor, she reminded them that fire is also a cleansing of the old and explains this is the root of 'spring cleaning'. Finally, she reminded everyone that the many handfasting ceremonies bind the loves, the powers, and the people to the seasons, the land, and to each other. By being bound together, they work and grow together in an unending cycle. A cycle, or a never-ending circle, is another form of protection as it is sealed and without any weakness for troubles to enter.

Then, speaking Old Fae, which most assumed was Ancient Gaelic, Joneya went through the ritualized movements and spoke the ancient words to bring health, growth, and prosperity through the land to the people, strengthening the protections against evil and troubles. She had done this every year from a distance, but this year she was here in person and the magic was palpable to everyone. Some old men thought the fire cider was awfully strong this year, some foolish girls thought the boys were especially handsome, and some few could swear they could see every living thing with an aura of energy around it. Those familiar with the land's energies felt almost drunk off the excessive, vibrant energy of the day. It steadily built through the blessing and then the handfasting ceremonies. Even Abaris could feel the heady excitement in the air, but he was willing to pass it off to the dark, foamy beer he had been drinking.

Finally, the parade wound to the Village. Excitement built in the children as they built the MayPole and the party. The excitement of the adults in their loins. The laughter in the eyes of the elderly as they looked to their loves and felt young again. Joneya's magic slipped into everyone, not just her own village, and the celebrations would be huge this year.

Beltane in the village was filled with music, dancing, food, and even a magician. Both Joneya's magic filled the air and the squeals of the audience as the other magician made coins disappear and pulled flowers from the air.

Eventually, much to their chagrin, the children are directed home. All the village children are sent home with sweet candies, fresh berries, balloons and ribbons. Young teens argue that they should stay, but all are met with the same fate as Joneya's children and sent home with chosen guardians.

"Let's find out just how pagan you are, my love?" she growls in Abaris' ear and pulls him away from the fire. "Luke will lead you to where I wait." She grabs a torch and runs ahead, with many of the older teens to middle-aged running after.

Luke brings a horn of cold beer to Abaris and tells him to drink deeply that he'll need it. Then Luke tells Abaris that they need to go quickly to meet Joneya. She knew he wouldn't want to run, but she wants him there for the full next ceremony. When he arrives, her clothes have gotten skimpier and there are torches set back from a clearing. He sees tall rocks at the 4 compass points each with a small torch or sconce. A horn of water is passed to Abaris, and he's told to take off his shirt, but to put the vest back on. His crown is straightened, and then Joneya beckons him in. She begins by kissing him deeply while the few who came with them pull back. Some couples slip away, other couples kiss just as deeply.

A drum starts beating rhythmically, like a heartbeat calling them. She breaks the kiss, whispers in his ear, "Follow my lead." She weaves them in a complex dance around the fire. He doesn't know the steps, but it doesn't matter. She has fancy footwork stomping the ground, almost like a jig, and tells him to make up his own steps. He's drunk enough to try. As soon as he starts dancing too, the couples still there start clapping and stomping in rhythm. Once they are back to the point they started, someone grabs Abaris' drink from him, and someone else grabs his hand. The dance continues, but the drumbeat speeds up. The crowd serpentines around the fire, dancing and sweating with their blood pounding in their heads, energy and sexual tension rising in their bodies. Suddenly, each couple breaks hands with the chain and whirls by themselves. "Jump with me," Joneya says.

"What?"

"Run and leap with me. As high as you can go." The bonfire is quite large, but being country kids, they know that simply jumping through the flames won't hurt. They'll feel the scorch of the heat, but they won't catch fire.

Together, grasping hands, Abaris and Joneya spin, run and leap over the highest point of the fire, stumbling a little on the landing on the other side. A strong hand grasps Joneya's free hand and helps steady her. Gasps run through the crowd as others follow them, jumping over the bonfire.

"The Stag!"

"The Stag King!"

"The Horned One!"

"The Great King is here!"

Joneya laughs out loud and grins. Locking arms instead of hands, Joneya, Abaris, and this handsome man in a crown matching Abaris' dance around the fire. After all the couples have jumped, they run and jump again over the highest point. A crescendo of drumming and stomping to match their leap.

Cold, heavy beer is handed to Abaris. Cold hard cider is handed to the crowned stranger and Joneya. Then the crowd parts and Abaris sees the woven hut for the first time. Joneya turns and the crowned stranger kisses her deeply. Breaking that kiss with a laugh, she turns and kisses Abaris just as deeply. His hand moves up her back. Pulling her head away, she nods towards the hut. The three of them move forward and duck into the hut as the drums pound.

"Trust me," Joneya whispers to Abaris. Then louder, "Cern, let me officially introduce you to Abaris, my mortal husband."

Cern's piercing green eyes met Abaris' hazel ones and said, "I'm grateful you came with her when she came home."

"Abaris, this is the Fae king, the Horned God, and so many other titles, not to mention a dear friend, Cern." Abaris held out his hand and shook. To Cern, she continued, "He's never done this ceremony before, so we need to explain a little."

"I think the actions need no explanation."

"Hmm," she nodded her agreement and kissed Abaris again, and began unlacing his vest. While she did so, Cern began untying the laces on her back. "This ceremony, as you know, is about the fertility and safety and strength of the land," she said against his lips. "But we also unite the two realms in this hut."

"You mean a threesome?" asked Abaris with a grin and a slight hitch of nerves.

"Uhhuh. Or a foursome. There's a wood nymph who would like to join us, but she knows that this might be overwhelming."

"Is there more beer?"

"There can be." Cern bit Joneya's neck playfully, then leaned through the woven curtain door and beckoned to someone. He leaned further out to talk to someone, and shortly, several bottles were handed in. Cern held open the woven drape of a door, and a slender woman slipped in. She knelt in front of Abaris and held out a hand. "You may call me Daphne."

"Daphne?" asked Abaris.

"Yes, that is the name that humans call me. My dryad name, or nymph name, is a sound of wind whistling through my leaves. It's too hard for you to pronounce."

"Daphne it is. I am very pleased to meet you." Abaris used his deep, gravely voice, and the sexual tension in the hut skyrocketed.

Daphne squeezed Joneya's hand in greeting and then she fully kissed Abaris, her hands soon clasped around his neck. Abaris went with the mood and kissed her back, confident that his wife was alright with it. He slid his hands up under her vest of a shirt. His strong hands moved up and down her back and then around her ribs, his thumbs just under her breasts. She didn't flinch and soon they found themselves with her sitting on his lap, and her hands moving down from his neck to open up and slip off his vest. Her palms rested for a minute on his powerful chest and then roved over his broad shoulders and thick arms.

Joneya and Cern were on their knees, Joneya beside Abaris and Cern beside Daphne. They had been kissing too, with hands exploring. Joneya and Cern were both shirtless, the torchlight gleaming off their sweaty skin and peaked nipples. Abaris felt a strange sensation on his head and went to remove his crown, rather than have it slip off.

Joneya grabbed his fingers, "No, it stays," she mumbled against his lips, then darted her tongue against his lips and then his teeth. His hand reached out and cupped her breast. He saw that her crown seemed to be small dancing flames and flowers woven into her hair. How could real fire possibly be in her hair? Cern leaned behind Joneya and kissed Daphne while stroking her cheek, then sliding his fingers through her hair. Suddenly, both women were flipped on their backs, with Abaris in front and Cern on his knees behind.

Abaris slid the rest of Daphne's clothes off and smoothly moved between her legs. His hands stroked up from her ankles to just above her knees. Then he held her eyes while his hands slid higher up her thighs. Seeing no hesitation, he leaned down and ran his lips and then his tongue up her left thigh, while his right hand moved lightly up her other. Fingers and mouth came together, and she gasped a little as he softly licked all around on her sensitive skin, gently tasting. She wiggled a little as he teased her. Then, deftly using both hands to gently pull open her lips, he licked her clit gently, then harder. She gasped and began breathing hard. Joneya knew exactly what Daphne was feeling. She knew that Abaris would deftly dance his tongue around, mostly on the utmost sensitivity, but occasionally moving down or out to intensify the feelings when he came back to focus solely on the clit.

Joneya had reached out to pull forth Cern's throbbing cock and slip it in her mouth. He groaned as her lips wrapped around him and her tongue pressed hard as she sucked. She ran one hand up across his hip and then up his ribs, her other hand around his other hip and cupped his ass, pulling him ever so slightly closer. Cern groaned more as she adjusted her angle and flicked her tongue over the head or around the edges of the foreskin.

Abaris never stopped working his tongue, firmly flicking now against Daphne's clit, and his thumb writing gentle swirls on her inner thigh, but he enjoyed watching Joneya pleasure Cern. He watched Cern kneeling, with his head thrown back, obviously enjoying the sensation. Then he watched as Cern pushed gently against Joneya's forehead, lifting her mouth away from his throbbing cock. "My turn," he said.

Abaris caught his eye and gave an approving nod as Cern moved to give Joneya the same teasing pleasure as Abaris gave to Daphne. Just as Cern began flicking his tongue against and away from Joneya's clit, Daphne arched her back and grabbed tight to Joneya's hand as she came. It was unlikely that any wood nymph had ever cum so hard. Abaris grinned in a self-satisfied way as he wiped his hand across his face. Cern and Joneya both smiled too until Cern distracted Joneya again with his magic tongue.

Daphne caught her breath and tried to quell her legs from shaking for a moment. Abaris laid down beside Daphne, still smirking. "Did you enjoy that?"

"Obviously," she laughed. She reached out then with one hand to grab and began to stroke his cock, which quickly sprang to life in her hand. She took another shuddering breath and then rolled over and used her other hand to trace intricate patterns against his skin.

"Don't tease me," Abaris breathed.

"Let me do this. They're sigils."

"They're what?"

Cern interjected quickly, "She's painting you with protective signs. You'll not come to any harm if the dryads can aid you in any way. Or they'll seek help for you. It's a great gift. Let her do it." He moved back then to giving Joneya his full attention and her closed eyelids fluttered at the intense feelings.

Before long there was mutual gratification amongst them all. Daphne rode Abaris, Cern plunged into Joneya as she rocked her hips under him matching his pace. Energy swirled through the hut, and it seemed like steam should be rising into the night air. Maybe it was. In an almost unbelievable coincidence, they all came within moments of each other. Cern throwing back his head and screaming into the night, his antlers glowing softly. They all sprawled back or on their side, gasping for breath. Abaris opened the bottles and gave them each a drink of deep red wine. He wasn't sure, but it tasted like blackberries - heavy and tartly sweet rolling back on his tongue.

After a few moments of quiet and heavy breathing, Joneya said to Abaris, "You do have the option of leaving the hut now. You can find someone else to play with or head home if you like."

"I'm in no hurry," He chuckled, "I'm not sure I could walk yet, anyway."

They all grinned. "You can, of course, stay," added Cern. "Most couples stay in the woods for quite a while before slipping home around dawn."

"It's not even the darkest part of the night, yet," added Daphne with a mischievous grin.

"I think that was a challenge!" Laughed Abaris as he rolled over and playfully grabbed her and she squealed.

# Chapter 4 - We Are Not The Same

"**I** need you to do this."

She still doesn't understand me, thought Joneya. Sir Ned's mask slipped for a split second with his raised eyebrow. Joneya laughed softly, "You perhaps misunderstand the difference between want and need. Understandable though, given your upbringing."

"My upbringing?! We grew up together!"

"Hardly," chuckled Joneya. Then she caught the look that Sir Ned gave her. How could he even give a look when his expression never changes? It must be the eyes. She briefly lifted her own eyebrows back at him in acquiescence. "Fine, let's not begin an argument." Joneya moved to the cupboard and removed a bottle of wine and two glasses. Sir Ned came over with a corkscrew in his hand. The man must have pockets like Hermione's bag in Harry Potter. Whatever it was called. "Sit, let's start again."

Queen Francesca took a deep breath and dropped onto the sofa. She didn't say anything, but biting back the cutting words was worth more than a "You're right."

Sir Ned opened the bottle and poured a glass for each of the sisters. He knew Joneya was right. The girls had grown up very differently, but Francesca really had no concept of the differences. She had been her mother's favorite and honestly hadn't noticed that she had the limelight and Joneya was in the background observing and interacting with the quiet powers while she, Francesca, flirted and smiled for the cameras. The differences went far deeper than being only half siblings.

"Sorry-"

"I'm sor-"

Both sisters smiled as they both apologized at once.

"Let's start again," said Joneya in a tired voice. She sipped her wine and leaned back in the overstuffed chair. They were in her library - built for comfort and reading, and not at all Francesca's style. But asking for help was Francesca's style, and they all knew that Joneya had the connections of all the people and both realms to arrange anything. Anything could be arranged or learned for a price. That was the part that Francesca forgot, never having had to pay for anything in her life. "What do you want?"

"I need you to look into an issue," started Francesca with a smile to take the bite out of the emphasis. "that I want to have resolved. I'm just not sure if it's serious or not, but I feel like it is."

Joneya lifted an eyebrow. "What issue? And how serious?"

"I don't know how serious it is. That's why I need you. It seems like just petty shit, but my gut says there is something more."

"Always listen to your gut." Joneya made a toasting gesture while she said it. Francesca lowered her eyes and looked down. They both remembered an incident with a certain young prince who had gotten a little too familiar. Both girls were uncomfortable with him, but while Joneya spoke with the guards and slipped a knife into her boot, Francesca played politics and flirted, happy for the eyes of the prince. It had ended bloody, quite literally, and the prince left quickly amid apologies from his aghast parents. Both girls learned that their gut had never steered them wrong, but Francesca carried the physical scars of the night, too. Carefully hidden, though they were.

"What's going on?" Joneya drank some more wine. Her gut was telling her this was important, and that she was about to get handed a mess to deal with.

"I know-we both know," started Francesca, "that drugs are bought and sold. You probably know who is selling them, too."

Joneya gave a quick nod. "Some of them."

"Uhhuh, they'll always be here. Just like there will always be power conflicts." Joneya held Francesca's eyes. They both knew that these were simple facts and just a part of life. The balance was kept by the rings of power moving around and through each other in harmony.

Joneya didn't say anything, just nodded.

"But someone is pushing and trying to disrupt the normal balance. Someone is trying to have more control, and it's bigger than the palace."

"Well, the whole town, hell, the entire country, is filled with an opioid crisis."

"No, I know that. The whole world, and I run programs for that-"

"That don't work, by the way."

"I know, but I'm trying. Just like you try to moderate it with your people."

"Yeah." Another sip of wine and Joneya refilled their glasses.

"Someone is trying to change the pattern. Someone is making a move. A big move."

"Yeah. Ok. I'll ask."

"Who are you going to ask?"

Joneya just looked at Francesca.

"Right." Francesca huffed a deep sigh. "I am the queen. I should know."

"Exactly why you shouldn't know." Joneya didn't even bother trying to sweeten her tone or choose gentler words. Part of who she was, was being completely straight and brutally honest. She had everyone's trust because they knew she would speak it straight and fair and treat everyone with equal respect unless they did something to betray her trust. She was the only one who could safely walk anywhere in the two kingdoms with criminals or law enforcement, upper class, lower class, with those with wings or four legs or fins. "Let's talk about something else. Is Castle Draug hosting a barbecue this year? A summer festival?"

Francesca immediately relaxed a tension she didn't know she was holding. "Yes, of course! I was thinking maybe for the solstice and you could co-host!"

"No." Joneya could think of nothing worse than hosting the Solstice with her sister. But before the word had even registered in the air, Joneya rethought it. "Well, maybe."

Francesca didn't say anything, and let her sister think. Apparently, she did follow her gut sometimes.

"Yeah, ok," Joneya agreed. "We have your hoity-toity get together, and some camera ready solstice activities, but also the real solstice celebration, too. Yeah, it could work." She smiled begrudgingly. "It's a good move."

Francesca genuinely smiled back. "Good. We'll make this happen. I want it to be right for both of us and all our people...er, citizens."

Joneya laughed, "Citizens! I'm not sure that's the right term for some of them." She swallowed another snort of laughter. "But, yeah."

Francesca gave a quick, happy clap of her hands. "Good! I'm sure we need a bonfire, and I thought a small maze for the children would be good for the cameras."

"Uhhuh," Joneya nodded, not quite as enthused.

"You make a list of what else you need and how we invite everyone-"

"I'll do our invites to the other realm," Joneya interrupted.

"Uhhuh, of course," continued Francesca. "And give me a list of who here in the village should have the very formal invites and who has less formal invites. It will be open to the public, of course."

"Parts of it."

"Yes."

"I can do that," agreed Joneya. "And planning this gives me the excuse to be at Draug and speak with people there, who may know your other little problem."

"Yeah."

***

The next day, true to her word, Joneya spent the morning at Castle Draug. The steward and the lead housekeeper were the obvious ones to speak with, but also the daily butler, the groomsmen, and even the guest housekeepers tend to overhear and observe a great deal. These are the staff that see the arguments and the tears, hear the praises, and come across (and tuck away) the private papers and evidences. They are the ones who must adapt to ever changing plans at a moment's notice. In a well-run household, the family and guests never even realize everything that the staff is providing for them and they hum along in the background. Decent people realize this and reward their staff accordingly.

Someone adept at politics, like Queen Francesca, relied heavily on the integrity and silence of her staff. She treated them with respect, openly thanking them for their services and trying to remember personal details of importance to their lives. In return, they showed her respect as well. But Joneya had done these decades before her sister and she had long-term relations with the majority of the staff. Every single staff member who worked in Castle Draug, or spoke with an older staff member of Draug, knew that they could approach Joneya and be heard with respect. She would then arrange what she could for them, at a price that they could afford (or in a way that mutually benefited them and another party). Queen Francesca was allowed to go anywhere on her property, but Joneya was welcomed with little to no formality everywhere on the property.

Joneya arrived in jeans, a spaghetti strap shirt, and a sweatshirt, wearing slip on sandals. Her guards had learned long ago that she dressed for comfort and movement, and they had learned to do the same. One never knew whether they would be standing in a public affair for hours, or traipsing through the woods, or shoveling manure from behind a barn to a garden. Joneya could and would do it all. In her sandals or barefoot. It was handy to have one of the guards on "shoe duty" to find her shoes and carry them in case they didn't return the same way. Joneya was more than comfortable everywhere barefoot, but some people rather frowned upon the informality in some locations. Likewise, the farmers and stable hands had given up on her wearing boots and allowed her in sandals. "Sandals or barefoot, but I won't complain for being stepped on." She brooked little argument and not a few of them had seen her stepped on by rowdy cows as she helped herd them, or an excited horse. She did agree to boots sometimes in a pig pen if she would be in it long - their teeth hurt.

Joneya entered Castle Draug from the back of the kitchens, but she was sure they were expecting her. Knowing she was coming might bring forth someone ready to talk. She stepped in and walked through like she owned the place, which she did in part. Like her, the bodyguards knew kitchen etiquette and yielded to the workers and said "behind" when moving behind someone in small quarters. They might be temporarily in the way, but they were never a nuisance. Sometimes, they even helped move a pot or load of something through the kitchen if they saw a need, or stopped to stir a pot if they had clean hands.

Today, Joneya had spoken to the guards before arriving and they found themselves a mug of tea and sat off to the side, out of the way. Joneya had her hair pulled back, tied her sweatshirt around her waist and slipped on an apron. Then, she stood by the Mistress of the Kitchens and peeled potatoes with her so she could talk. They neither spoke loudly for all to hear, nor in hushed, secret voices.

"What's the good word today, Chef?" asked Joneya as she glanced over to see how the potato was being sliced after peeling. Quarter inch rounds, apparently.

"Ahh, nothing exciting, but it's a sunny day here, MLady." Chef Erin knew better than to waste her breath telling Joneya not to work. Indeed, it was easier this way. They both needed busy hands, and the work had to be done. Also, it was easier to have a conversation side by side while working than while facing each other sipping tea.

"The Summer Solstice party/barbeque/shindig. What do you need from me?" asked Joneya.

"Ahhh, lass, I've no idea, yet," laughed the Mistress. "You let me know if you have a special request, and I'll let you know what help we need as we figure it out."

"Yup." The answer surprised neither of them, but it did start the simple conversation. Chef Erin surprised her then.

"I expect you're here about the troubles."

Joneya lifted an eyebrow and glanced at her, but kept peeling. "I may be. Something like that anyway. What can you tell me?"

The cook bit her lip in thought. "I'll tell you quick what I do think. I was going to send a lass over to ye today to talk. But I'll have you talk directly to a few of the help here, rather than me gossiping about what I've heard." She gave a questioning look to Joneya to see if she agreed.

"Yeah." Joneya nodded. It made sense to have the information directly rather than second hand and they both knew it. "How many potatoes will this take?"

Chef Erin laughed, "About this many. But your boys may need some bread and jam to soak up all the tea they'll be drinking."

Joneya chuckled, too. "Maybe some of your cookies. They like my chocolate chip, but you have the magic hand."

"I taught you all I know."

"Maybe I'm just not that good a learner."

"I've actually heard good things about your cookies."

Joneya just snorted a laugh. "Ok shoot, and tell me what you know."

"Hmm, well, what I know is little, but I'll tell you some of what I suspect, too. Then you'll speak with that red-haired lass by the stove." She nodded her head to point over, and the girl looked up and met Joneya's eyes. Joneya smiled and nodded her head. The girl jumped a little and went back to diligently stirring the pot. She wasn't a girl that Joneya knew, though she recognised her face. The Mistress of the Kitchens did know her by name and would not allow her to slack off just because Joneya was looking at her.

Joneya talked a few more minutes with Chef Erin, the Mistress of the Kitchens of Castle Draug, then Joneya went over to speak with the red haired lass by the stove

The poor girl seemed nervous as Joneya came closer, and she paused her stirring of the enormous pot just long enough to wipe her face.

"Hey, you look awfully uncomfortable," Joneya said with a smile. "I want to chat with you a bit. Chef Erin said you might have some information that could help me, but why don't you go wash your face and get a cool drink first. I'll stir the pot for you for a moment."

"Oh no, m'Lady, I couldna do that." The poor girl was already beet red from the heat, so she couldn't possibly blush any redder.

"Of course you can. And don't make me issue a royal decree or something." Joneya was joking, but the poor girl didn't seem sure. "Go ahead, lass. What's your name, by the way?"

"Everyone calls me Sissy, m'Lady," mumbled the poor girl.

"Alright, Sissy," smiled Joneya, "I'll follow everyone's cue. Go take a break for a moment, while I stir this for you." She leaned over the pot and pulled in the aroma. "Oh my Goddess, this stew smells amazing, Sissy. I know this isn't Chef Erin's recipe!"

"Umm, no, m'Lady." She ducked her head while speaking so softly that Joneya could hardly hear her. "It's me family's recipe, it's quite popular in the Tavern." She turned abruptly then and almost ran from the kitchen.

Joneya leaned over the pot again and took a deep whiff. She didn't even particularly like stew, but she knew that this was something special. Tavern, tavern? Is there one in the village that's known for its lunch? Maybe it's a stew? Wait, something about a pot that's always ready to serve. It IS a pot of stew! Now which tavern is it? The Broken Hammer, no. It's not the Goat's Maid. McGiully's? Maybe...The Charred Axe! That's it. I wonder if that's her family?

Sissy took a little while to return to the kitchen, but when she came back her cheeks were a pretty pink and she looked much calmer.

"Sissy, I have to tell you, well I don't have to, but I'm going to tell you," chuckled Joneya, "I don't like stew. Like at all. But this stew smells really, really good."

"Really, m'Lady?" asked Sissy with a shy, dimpled smile. "Thank you, m'Lady."

"Hush now, let's be less formal. We're both sweating in the kitchen. We can certainly drop that hard "L" of m'Lady."

"Umm, alright m'La-m'lady," stuttered Sissy.

"That's better," Joneya smiled warmly and rubbed her arm across her face to wipe off some of the sweat. "Now I understand that there have been troubles happening at the castle and maybe ye can help me solve them."

"Ahh, no, m'lady," Sissy turned red again. "I'm sure I can't help you."

"I'm sure you can, Sissy." Joneya sighed loudly. She wanted to rub her temples and her neck, but that wasn't appropriate in the kitchen. "Look, all I know is that there is something going on, but I have no idea what the hell it is. I need at least some clues although some actual evidence would be even better. So help me out here, Sissy. What do you know?"

Sissy bit her lip.

"Look, Sissy, I know you don't know me, but I will protect you. You can ask around, if you like. Unless you're planning on killing a member of the royal family, I won't tell anyone what you've told me. And I'll be talking with others to see what they have observed." Sissy's shoulders lowered a little, and the tension began to leave her face. She raised her clear, green eyes up to Joneya's. "No one needs to know what you've said versus what I learned elsewhere. We can talk somewhere else, if you don't want to talk in the kitchen. Or, you can always send a message to me, too, if you think of something else."

"Yes, mum." Sissy took a deep breath and reached a decision. "I'll talk to you here, mum."

"Good." Joneya smiled warmly.

Joneya spent the day at Castle Draug observing interactions between staff, listening to others while pretending to read through paperwork (airpods are great for this - amazing what people may say when they don't think you can hear them) and generally walking quietly through the halls and secret passages. She also spent time listening to anyone that would talk to her.

There were red cheeks and whispers about who was dating whom, who had cheated on whom, and Joneya just wanted to roll her eyes at the drama. Until she came upon a maid crying in the seldom used rose dining room. The room was decorated in an over-enthusiastic interpretation of the theme with roses added onto or rose-colored everything. Even the gorgeous stone fireplace had been painted a hideous shade of dusty rose. The poor maid was a thorn in the theme, dressed all in black, but giving the eye a welcome break.

Joneya didn't say anything as she stepped into the room and saw the poor girl crying. She was slumped by the window, staring out at the pasture. Joneya simply came up and leaned against her back, slipping her arms around her. The maid sank back and soaked up the hug for a minute. She turned to say something, and a cry of alarm erupted from her throat as she leapt to her feet.

"Hush now," Joneya soothed, but she stepped back to give the young lady space. "Every woman, every human, should offer solace and comfort when they can."

"Oh no, M'Lady!" The poor maid started crying again, but a completely different sound. She no longer sounded heartbroken, but now sounded terrified. "M'Lady, I should have been working, not sitting! I'm sorry. It shan't happen again! I swear. Oh please, my Lady, don't fire me-"

Joneya cut her off, shaking her head and speaking softly, "Don't you think every single person in this castle has had a need to lay their head down and take a moment to sort their feelings? Of course they have. I'll never be upset with you for having feelings. I promise you that."

"But-but the queen-" the maid stuttered.

"The queen isn't really so bad as to fire you for having an off day either, is she?" Joneya paused and the maid hesitantly shook her head. "And, if she ever is that sort of person, then you leave here with your head held high and come to House Isilme and ask to speak with me. If I'm not there, you speak to any of my staff and they will make sure you have a hot meal and a bed until I can arrive." Seeing the maid still looking hesitant, Joneya added, "Who do you take care of?"

"Take care of, m'Lady?" asked the maid, confused.

"Uhhuh. Take care of." Joneya managed to be serious and friendly in her tone simultaneously. "Someone is dependent on you working. Who do you take care of?"

"But how did you-" She paused and flushed again at Joneya's raised eyebrow. "Yes, mum. I take care of me younger brother and me gram. We live together and me wages provide most everything for us."

"Ok," smiled Joneya as she motioned to the chair. "Sit, please. I'll make sure that no matter what you tell me right now, that your brother and your gram are seen after, even if I have to move them into my house. No, that won't be necessary, I'm sure, but they'll be taken care of. I promise. Now, I need two things from you."

"Yes, m'Lady?"

"Come now, we can drop a little of the formality. Let's just chat." Joneya sat down beside her, but not too close. She patted the maid's hand, but then withdrew her own to be less imposing. "I need to know why you're crying and I need to know about The Troubles."

The maid gasped, and her face blanched.

"Are they the same?" asked Joneya softly.

"Maybe, mum." The maid looked down at her hands now clasped in her lap. "I dunno, maybe." Tears slid down her cheeks again, and she kept twisting the ring on her finger.

"Ok." Joneya spoke softly and calmly. She let her calm permeate the room, and she watched the maid's shoulders loosen and relax. The tension left her face, her eyes softened. Then Joneya spoke softly, "Start how you want. With that ring, maybe."

The maid looked up, her eyes red and desperate, "You're going to fix this, aren't you, m'Lady?"

Joneya took in a deep breath and held it for a moment. She released a pent up breath, "Yeah." She rubbed her forehead a moment and squeezed the bridge of her nose as she took another deep breath. "Fuck. I don't know what "this" is, but yeah, I'm gonna fix it."

The maid gave a small smile. "Yeah, you are." She shook her head in wonder. "You're the only one who can."

"Fuck." Joneya breathed the word out. This was exhausting. "Ok, tell me."

# Chapter 5 - Another Country Heard From

Joneya dropped herself into the back seat of the SUV next to Sir Ned. He handed her a glass of wine as she slipped her shoes off. He must have known she needed some emotional healing because Sere was there too and dropped his heavy head on her lap. Long practice kept her wine glass above the rottweiler's head. Sir Ned let her sip and lean her head back with her eyes closed for the first few minutes.

When she had recomposed herself, or pushed past a little of the exhaustion, she turned her head, opened an eye and lifted an eyebrow in question.

"Alright, lass, where do ye wish to start?"

She closed her eyes again. "With a nap," she muttered. Not quite as quietly as she intended, because Sir Ned chuckled. She sat up, with eyes wide open, and rubbed Sere's head, just behind his ears. "Yup, all of it. However you want to share it." She sipped some more wine, but gave Sir Ned her full attention.

"The Troubles as they're calling it seems apt," he said stoically. "There seem to be quite a few pockets of Troubles. Some of it is the fair normal drama, just being lobbed in with the other, but there are some strange occurrences and coincidences. What the guards sniffed out is similar to what you've been told by the otherworlders at The Cottage. But more than just a ...magical disturbance, there seems to be someone or a group of someones riling up the lower staff, not just at the castle, but some other high houses, too."

"Yeah," Joneya swallowed the last of the glass of wine, but shook her head against more. "It's like someone, or a group of someones, are stirring the pot to create enough discord to cause a minor rebellion. But I can't figure out what the "cause" is or what the rebellion is actually rebelling against."

Sir Ned nodded his agreement, but didn't say anything.

Joneya continued, "And, there's always drama of a who is dating whom and some nobility in love with a servant and vice versa, but it seems like the drama has been hitched up a notch or two."

Sir Ned pondered this, "You're right. I was discounting the drama, as you will, but you're right, it seems a little heavier than normal." He paused for a moment and then continued, "I may have been remiss. I was told that some of the help had gone missing. But I thought it was just that they quit and moved on without announcing their plans."

Joneya sat straight up. "Wait, really? Sorry." She tilted her head with a slight grimace smile, acknowledging the ridiculousness of her question. "I mean, there's a groom missing too, from the castle. There's a maid quite upset about it. Maybe she's right that he wouldn't have just left as it seems he did."

Sir Ned nodded as she spoke. Neither of them wasted time berating themselves for not catching the potential clue before.

"I need your men to look into the missing people more." Handle it however you think best, whether openly or quietly."

Sir Ned nodded his agreement and added, "We'll see what other Houses have missing members, too."

"Yeah," Joneya rubbed her temples, and Sere thumped her tail in solidarity. "I'll be going to The Cottage tomorrow."

"Aye. That's another thing I have to tell you. A letter was left at the House. The Mermaids need a meeting with you. They said you know where to find their spokesperson."

Joneya's eyebrow lifted and dropped, and she bit her lip. "Uh-huh." She took another deep breath in through her nose and held it a moment while thinking. "I'll write a response tonight, and if you're willing, we'll deliver it in the morning. Depending on what they want, we might just leave the note or we might converse."

Sir Ned nodded. "Just let me know when you're ready to go." After a moment, he added, "She's switched out some books from the Cottage, I think. The boys don't know her, but they've reported that a woman comes every few days and exchanges books. I assume it's her."

"Hmm." Joneya smiled a little at that. Then she leaned her head back for the last couple minutes of the ride and rubbed Sere's head. She wasn't sure who was comforting whom, but it seemed to be mutually beneficial. Goddess, she hated politics!

As always, please turn the thumb blue so I know you enjoyed this episode, and I would be grateful if you would share your crown with me. Have a day!

"Another country heard from?" asked Abaris, as Joneya sealed her letter. As promised, she had written a response to the mermaid summons the night before, but she hadn't had the energy to find an envelope.

"Almost literally. More 'another world', but they're here too." She paused, but he was sitting quietly and giving her his full attention. He had seen too much to just discount this as foolishness. "There are multiple worlds or universes or realms, however you want to think of it. They exist independently for the most part, and oblivious to the others, except that at certain points there's thinness, or a space, that they all occupy simultaneously."

"And this is one of those spots that the planes intersect?"

"Yeah."

"Of course it is." He pondered for a moment, then swallowed some tea and asked, "All of here is, or the Cottage is?" He distinctly remembered going with her to The Cottage and meeting some characters who were...otherworldly if anyone was.

"It's this general area," she smiled, remembering how well he had handled that first visit and encountering subjects with purple eyes, or wings, or just weirdness about them. "The Cottage is a place that they all feel safe approaching. Most of them will not come here where there are a lot of humans. Some of them cannot come here because of the wards-"

"Wards?" he asked.

"Umm, wards are like magical padlocks and fences. We use them to keep out some of the more dangerous people, but some people have keys."

"Do I even want to know?"

She laughed softly. "Remember the bedtime stories of magical creatures I tell the kids?"

"...yeah."

"Uhhuh. Truth is stranger than fiction. They understand too. Vampyres tend to ward their own homes, too."

"Fuck me."

"Now that," she grinned, "sounds like fun." She giggled as she dropped the letter down and came over to straddle his lap."

"Aren't you supposed to be meeting Sir Ned this morning?" Abaris asked against her lips pressed to his.

"Uhhuh, but not for a little while." She bit his lower lip gently and added, "now hush." Her lips moved down to his neck, grazing her teeth against his pulse and then flicking her tongue against the skin. She sucked hard for a moment and then licked her way to the front of his neck, right where the collar of his shirt opened. Her hands meanwhile slid under his shirt and grazed against his stomach and along the sides. She gently ran her nails against his skin and felt goosebumps rise.

He slid his hands under her shirt and up her back. Thick, powerful hands with roughened skin and her skin goose bumped, too. Their breathing had shortened, their eyes smoldered and were heavy lidded. Joneya and Abaris craved each other like a thirsty man craved cool water. His hands moved to her sides, his thumbs against her stomach, and he pushed her back. As she leaned back, he leaned forward and kissed her hard on the mouth. Their tongues danced like flames, and their touches seared. Like she had done, his mouth moved to a kiss on the corner of her mouth and then traced along her jaw and towards her neck. His voice, deepened with arousal, whispered against her ear. "Let's go somewhere more comfortable."

It was a question and yet more a statement. Abaris had felt the heat between her legs as she had sat on his lap, pressed up against his own heat. His core screamed to plunge into her, and he knew she craved it just as much. As she laughed softly, deep in her throat, she slid off of him and offered him a hand to stand. Their fingers locked as they moved to their bedroom, miraculously meeting no one.

Abaris stood beside the bed as Joneya knelt upon it. They kissed, those lighter, exploratory kisses with tongues touching and jumping, nibbles on lips, and hot breath shared. They both slid hands under shirts and lifted the shirts up. She let go first, slipping her arms out of her shirt as he lifted it over her head. Then she reversed roles and slid her hands back against his hot skin and lifted his shirt. Her mouth followed her fingers and as the shirt covered his face, she teased his nipple with her tongue, flicking it. It hardened immediately, and he growled.

Abaris pushed her back onto the bed and undid the button on the front of her pants. She lifted and wiggled her butt to help him slide her pants off. He paused then, marveling at the morning sunlight dancing over her body. Joneya did not have a perfect body, but she was beautiful. He kissed her belly as his hands slid down to her hips. Abaris rubbed his rough chin against her soft skin, and her breathing hitched. Then, his tongue flicked down to follow where his beard had been.

Joneya's skin was on fire and the blood roared in her ears. She couldn't help herself. Her back arched as his tongue blazed his way to her core. Her breathing was broken by a gasp and the world momentarily rushed and stopped as she released herself completely to the feelings. Abaris' hands held her hips still as she started to thrash and he didn't stop until her breathing slowed and her hands touched his and she slid back a little. He grinned at her while he wiped his face. Then he climbed over her, caging her between his strong arms and legs. She reached down and stroked his cock through his jeans, fumbling with the button until she finally freed it and unzipped his pants. Joneya slid one hand in to stroke through his boxers, and he caught his breath. She brought up one foot to hook her toes into his waistband and used her hand on the other side to slide down his pants. He wiggled and then helped her remove his boxers, too.

Abaris leaned against Joneya, his hot, throbbing cock against her, his mouth glued to hers. Then she opened her legs wide and guided him in. Welcoming and surrounding him with her heat. He groaned again as he was enveloped in squeezing, hot, softness. Abaris slowly slid in, and just as slowly, pulled back. Joneya hated this slow pace, and he knew it. She suffered through the painfully slow delight for a couple strokes, lifting her hips slightly to take him deep within. Then, wanting to wait no more, she began to move under him, meeting his thrusts and pulling back herself. Together they crashed into each other, plunging deep and pulling back, grinding his pelvis against her clit. Their mouths danced together and then breathing became too difficult and they pressed cheek to cheek; her hands sliding over her shoulders, along his sides, and teasing a nipple. Higher and higher they followed the thrusts, the rising energy until the world thundered around them and outward like an explosion of energy. Indeed, it was. Rings of that energy widened and spread out, feeding the land and energizing the people. Just as powerful as Beltaine, Joneya harnessed the powers of the universe to nourish the land, her people, the realms. And then they lay there panting.

Abaris rolled a little, shifting his weight off of Joneya, but their legs still intertwined. "Did you like that?"

Joneya laughed, completely happy and satisfied in the moment.

A soft knock came at the door. They groaned in unison.

"Just a moment," called Joneya. Then quieter, she said, "fuck. I want to just stay right here."

"I'm sorry, Alder. I need you." Sir Ned paused a half second. "I need both of you."

"Shit!" The use of her royal codename signaled the urgency. "Coming."

Abaris began pulling on his pants. Joneya grabbed a throw blanket, wrapping it around herself as she rushed to the door. Sir Ned met her eyes as he stepped through the door as soon as he could fit. She breathed out a little at his gaze. It was urgent, but not horrible. He stepped in and then pointedly turned around so she could dress. She dropped the blanket and listened as she pulled on clothes.

"I'm sorry to barge in, but the safety of your family is paramount." Sir Ned stood in a relaxed stance, but the tension was evident in his shoulders and how he held his head.

"Of course," said Joneya and Abaris together.

"We have received not one, but two credible threats this morning-"

Abaris interrupted, "Two?"

Sir Ned didn't bat an eye, but continued to speak calmly in a clipped, informative tone. "Yes, two credible threats. It's not uncommon for the royal families to receive threats, but most are deemed irrelevant. Sometimes we heighten security while we look into it, but these seem to warrant more."

"While we might assume that you are the primary target, Joneya, that wasn't specifically given. Thus, we must consider that it would be more damaging to your psyche to have your family in danger than yourself, and act accordingly."

Joneya half smiled. It was true; she cared far more about any risks to her husband and children, even her dog, than to herself. "Yeah." She nodded her understanding. "So what do we know, and what do you need?" The first half of the question would allow her to plan for the eventualities. The latter part of the question was what did the security teams need immediately to keep her family safe. She wouldn't waste time arguing about protocols or plans. Not now, not for the next several hours and maybe days. "You can turn now."

Sir Ned spun around at her words and gave her a tight smile. "We have already increased perimeter monitoring, and I have called more guards in. We'll double our numbers for every shift. We will try to keep the appearance that life is normal here, but I insist that you stay on the property."

Joneya nodded. It was what she had expected. "The children's adventures will be restricted to closer to the house. Perhaps we could have some friends over for them to play."

Sir Ned nodded his approval. Keeping the children closer to the house meant it was easier to protect and faster to retreat if necessary. Further, he saw the slight frown and understood she was using her political intelligence, too. Children from the other royal families being here would protect her own children if it were the other royal families who were making the threats. They would not risk their own heirs.

"Do we know which realm the threat comes from?"

Abaris' eyebrows jumped at the question, but he didn't say a word. He had seen some "people" from the other realms at The Cottage.

"No. We do not."

"I see. Then, we still meet with the Mer representative."

"I thought you would feel that way." Sir Ned didn't share his stresses, it was his job. Normally only he and Joneya went to the Murky Pond and thus kept the secrets of the place. But today he would need extra protection ahead and with them.

"We have allies, Sir Ned. We'll have to trust someone while we move through this. I'll request an escort from the Centaurians."

Sir Ned let out a breath of air he didn't know he had been holding. "Yes, they will work. I trust them."

Joneya snorted. Her house might be the only ones who "trusted" the Centaurians, but trust them, they did.

As expected, Joneya's request for a Centaurian escort was immediately granted. As Joneya and Sir Ned stepped out of the house, they were joined by two tall, very tanned, brown-haired men. They didn't say anything, but shook hands with Sir Ned and subtly showed him the brand on their wrists. They were of the Cheiron tribe. As they all set off down the path to the back of the property, the Centaurians' muscular legs outpaced them, and they were soon about thirty paces off ahead and behind.

As they came closer to Murky Pond, the birdsongs returned. Joneya looked at Sir Ned and raised an eyebrow. He met her eyes and lifted his in return. Neither had noticed the lack of bird noises until they were suddenly hearing them again. They passed horses grazing the tall meadow grass. Joneya spoke soft greetings to them as they passed by.

As they walked, Sir Ned shared more intel from what they would normally have in their morning meetings. "It seems that there has not only been a rise in people just not showing up for their jobs, but also in the frequency of bribes. Even the rumors of blackmail have risen."

"I feel like we're holding on just by luck and the skin of our teeth. What the hell happened and how did we miss it?"

"I think," Sir Ned paused somberly and chose his words with care. "I think neither you, nor your sister, can be held accountable for these Troubles starting. Your mother was not known for staying connected to the land nor of the common people. I think, perhaps, the roots took place during her reign and now we are seeing the growth. There is no excuse that I did not see, but I think you and your sister inherited this issue."

"Sir Ned," scolded Joneya, "If you are to blame for not seeing it begin, then so is my sister - she was here, and so am I - for not being here. There's no blame to lay."

"Hmm. And do you honestly feel that?"

"That you're not to blame? Absolutely!"

"And that you hold no blame?"

"Ahh, well. As to that." Joneya smiled grimly, "I never was good at delegating anything away."

"Truth be that." SIr Ned snorted again.

They rounded the last bend then and almost stopped short, continuing to walk with only a slight hesitation. She was waiting for them, reclining in the water to keep her scales wet. When they were close enough so they could hear without her raising her voice, she said, "I know the horseman aren't here to protect you from me." Her lip curled in distaste. "So why are they here, polluting near my waters?"

Joneya bit the inside of her cheek. She hadn't thought of that. "Mm, I hadn't considered that. I'm sorry." She dipped her head to the woman, truly meaning what she said. "I hadn't considered the pollution. I just needed a party this morning whom I could trust."

The woman's eyebrows lifted in surprise. That was happening a lot this morning. "Trust them for what?" Her voice was reminiscent of old wooden oars moving in a rowboat. Neither smooth nor rough, but rustically splintered. Care was needed to avoid a wayward splinter under the skin, but beautiful in their own right. She moved up and stepped out of the water, two long legs where a scaled tail had been only moments before.

"We received a threat at the House, but it was important that I come to see you anyway," Joneya spoke calmly. The woman's nostrils flared, as if smelling for deception on the wind. Finally, she nodded. "In part, that might be why we want to speak."

Joneya and Sir Ned sat on the boulders near the merfolk woman. Joneya exchanged a book for a cup of tea offered by her. Sir Ned simply nodded his thanks and sipped his tea. There was no tea blend on dry land quite like it.

"Let's enjoy our tea quietly for a moment, before we disrupt ourselves with unpleasant talk. Though I assure you, I mean no harm to you or your family."

Joneya used all her restraint to keep her face still. The woman laughed outright then. "Ye have gotten better at that, m'Lady."

Even Sir Ned coughed against his tea, and Joneya's mouth twitched into a smile.

# Chapter 6 - Red Sky In The Morning

After sipping their tea quietly with the mermaid for a few minutes, Joneya and Sir Ned turned their gazes from the water's edge to her face. She hissed as if burnt and slipped a foot into the lapping waves just at her feet.

"Did you," she began in that creaky boat voice, "happen to notice how red the sky was this morning?"

Joneya shook her head. Her mind had otherwise been occupied, and she didn't go out at dawn today. Sir Ned shook his head, too.

"Indeed, the sky was blood red at sunrise. Some say that ought to mean "'heed warning'."

"Red at night-sailor's delight, red in the morning-sailors take warning?" rhymed Sir Ned. Joneya simply waited.

"There seem to be three factions amongst the otherworlders right now." Suddenly speaking quickly, the merwoman's tone had changed. "There are those who hold no interest in this world or you. There are those who fear you or hate you, and plot endlessly against you. And the third faction are those who support you, even defend you." She nodded her head towards the centaurians in the grasses.

Joneya simply nodded her head. It had never been spoken out so simplistically, but she knew at its root, the merwoman spoke true.

"Do you know," asked the woman, her smile changing to a snarl, "which faction seems to be growing?"

"No." Joneya kept her tone even. She knew that this merwoman could kill her in seconds if she chose. Her lengthening teeth and snarling voice evidenced her anger. But, Joneya trusted her. Joneya trusted only a few people: Abaris, Sir Ned, and only a handful of others.

"The third faction seems to be working hard to gather as many of the neutrals as they can. It seems they are making many promises for the neutrals to cross planes and cause you problems here. Especially the elves."

"The elves?" asked Sir Ned. If his eyes hadn't widened slightly, Joneya might not have recognized his surprise. The merwoman could smell it.

"Indeed." She took a breath and swirled her toes in the water. After a moment, her razor-like teeth started to recede. "They even seem to be kidnapping some residents of this plane."

"Indeed?" Sir Ned snapped his fingers.

"That explains some of the disappearances." Joneya nodded at Sir Ned, but turned again to the merwoman to ask, "But why? What are they upset about and coming over to kidnap my people here?"

"The people are pawns." The merwoman was indifferent to most humans. "They're pointless."

"I'm not sure that their families would agree," suggested Joneya.

The merwoman shrugged. "Mayhap you want to just worry about your own family. As they succeed, they get braver."

"So, what do they want?" asked Joneya. Sir Ned was on high alert and the centaurians had moved closer, perhaps sensing the stress levels rising.

"They want your empathy, methinks. But they are like dragons and their emotions are pulled only by power."

"What?" Joneya could feel the headache looming, but she couldn't smooth the creases from her brow. She did purposely loosen her shoulders. The day had started with such promise.

"They want your...mmm empathy isn't the right word, but neither is love." The merwoman looked equally stressed. "The factions are uniting that have never united before. They see you as a common foe. Not an enemy, but someone who must be brought to the reeds." She paused, then continued, "All the built up frustrations of the past centuries are being blamed on you. Or laid for you to fix, more aptly because your Queen Mother made some of those errors."

"Fuck me." Joneya sighed and pinched the bridge of her nose. "Thank you." After another long breath, she said, "What else do I need to know?"

"They will keep coming until they have your attention." She paused. "I think you need to go to them in their realm to gain their full respect."

"Yeah."

"Don't be foolhardy, no matter how they escalate. Know your boundaries and follow the rules and the customs. Do NOT endanger yourself in their power. Do NOT place yourself at their mercy. They have no reason to grant any."

"No reason? I do actually send them a bit of power-"

"Some reason," agreed the merwoman. "But not enough. They are emotional enough to say none. I don't know how long I can hold back my people." She admitted the last with downcast eyes. It was a huge admission.

"The merfolk, too?"

"They are part of the many who are upset," agreed the merwoman, speaking of her people. "They have found that your people's world often confuses money for power and that is their doorway in."

"Ok," Joneya chewed her bottom lip.

The merwoman hissed in frustration, "You do not understand!"

"Not entirely, no," agreed Joneya, "but I'm listening."

The merwoman tilted her head back. "Aye, you are not your mother. We must needs remind the others of this. I think that must be at the root of your next step. Show them you care, even though you don't understand."

"Suggestions?" asked Sir Ned in a quiet voice. He seldom spoke during a meeting like this, and today he had been almost chatty.

The merwoman looked at him with a raised eyebrow, but she respected him enough to answer. "Our lady will have to figure this one out. But you must protect her." She paused and then continued as she walked backward into the water, "Always keep her in the palm of your hand, boy, as they try to snatch her away."

Sir Ned and Joneya stood there, deep in thought, as the ripples from the merwoman disappeared. Then, in the distance, back at House Isilme, a bell began to toll. As one, they turned to the path and ran. Not more than twenty steps into their sprint, two centaurians came alongside them, shimmered and then offered their broad horse backs. Joneya grabbed the bottom of the mane and pulled herself up, bareback, onto his strong shoulders. The centaurian leapt forward, his long strides eating up the path, and soon House Isilme peeked into sight.

The Hand and the Hidden Queen were met at the gate by House Isilme's guards. Speaking to them both, a trusted guard said, "The Centaurians are reinforcing the perimeter. All the children are inside and with tripled guards from our house, Mariella is in with them."

"Abaris?" interrupted Joneya.

"Mum, I'm sorry, we don't know what happened."

"Explain," snapped Sir Ned.

"The wards rang, but when we went to investigate, it was apparent that there had been a scuffle in the room, but no one had heard anything. We cannot locate your husband, M'Lady."

Joneya shut her eyes to dissipate the heady, gray spots in front of her eyes. But she didn't react more than that outwardly. She knew, just as well as the two men and the two centaurians beside her, that they were being watched. There would be time for tears or throwing things later. Sir Ned was there beside her, close enough to reach out, but he didn't touch her.

To the two centaurians Joneya said, "Thank you. You saved me precious time. I won't forget your help." To Sir Ned and the guard, she said, "With me." Joneya paced herself, moving calmly into the house, but then hurrying down the halls to the children's wing. Still out of sight from their rooms, she slowed and took a deep breath. Then she and the men strolled down to their rooms. Joneya stood in the doorway and looked in. Several guards met her eyes, but didn't say anything. Mariella gave her a quick nod in greeting, but kept reading the book she was holding. The tv blared with "Teen Titans" and all seemed normal. Joneya smiled and stepped back, then she hurried down the hall to the stairs at the middle of the house. The first two floors, these were just normal stairs. But on the upper levels, these stairs were seldom used. They led to the Widow's Peak or the Widow's Walk, despite the house being far from the ocean.

However, just like the houses built on the shore, one could climb to the roof and stride its length back and forth while looking out into the distance. Joneya wasn't sure what to look for, certainly not a ship with full sails, but she knew she would recognize it when she did see it. She quickly scanned the close grounds and then set her eyes to the outskirts of the fields and trees.

"There," she said softly, nodding in the direction.

Sir Ned nodded and brought his binoculars closer to examine the spot.

"Shit," said the guard. Who then turned scarlet for swearing in his queen's presence.

"Indeed," agreed Joneya.

It would be easy to miss, but there was the slight flickering at the edge of the trees. There shouldn't be any portals or doorways on her property except a heavily guarded one by The Cottage. Yet somehow, through and past all of Joneya's wards, there was indeed the telltale flicker of a magic doorway. As she looked through the binoculars, she saw a robed figure standing just under the trees. Apparently, they could see her as well. Her eyes focussed on that ruby robed figure, and they -Joneya couldn't tell if they were male or female- stepped closer to the doorway. They lifted their left arm, open palm up, and shot a cloud of deep purple sparks into the sky. Then they spun, robe twirled out around them, and lept through the doorway. Just as they passed through the flicker and disappeared, they twisted and threw another set of sparks and this time straight towards the manor house.

"Down!" yelled Sir Ned at the same time Joneya dropped and pulled the guard down with her.

The purple splashed over an invisible dome above the house, creating the effect of fireworks between them and the blue sky. The sparks snapped and popped against that invisible dome and then sputtered out. Three heads snuck looks again over the wall of the Widow's Walk, but nothing unusual was visible now. No flicker, no purple smoke, and no scarlet robed figure.

"Medium build, average height, slender arm and hand," stated Sir Ned.

"Uhhuh," agreed Joneya. "The sparks weren't powerful, but whoever broke the wards to open the doorway and to keep it open was strong. Very strong."

"Hair color, feeling, anything else?" asked Sir Ned.

"Good eyes, I had only just seen them when they moved from hiding towards the portal. It was like they waited until I had just seen them." Then Joneya added, "And they knew I would come up here. Knowledge of warfare tactics or knowledge of me?"

"Uhhmm," Sir Ned said, "Did you notice anything about the robe?"

"It was red, but that may or not mean anything," Joneya held her bottom lip between her teeth as she thought. "I couldn't see any emblems or insignia. I didn't see any rings or bracelets. No belt about the robe or chain hanging around their neck over the robe. Purple sparks don't mean anything to me either, except showing off."

"OK then," Sir Ned nodded towards the door. "Inside Alder, there's nothing more for you out here."

"But-"

"No." The gravelly voice was soft, but harder than any marble or obsidian wall.

Joneya's nostrils flared, actually flared, in pent up irritation, but she didn't say a word. Sir Ned seldom ushered her to any sort of safety, so when he did, she could hardly argue.

"Fuck me," she mutter as she spun on her heel and strode to the door.

Sir Ned rolled his eyes to the sky and followed. His queen was brilliant, brave, and headstrong, but she wasn't stupid or completely obstinate like her mother.

At the bottom of the stairs, Joneya almost stomped her way to her study, but turned at the last moment to the private library next to her quarters instead. Sir Ned wouldn't let her be in a room with ground floor exterior access. Sir Ned asked a servant to send up some coffee and followed her in.

"Where the fuck is he?" she growled.

"We'll figure it out."

She narrowed her eyes at him, but they both knew it wasn't him that she was angry at. "Fuck, she knew, didn't she? The cunt knew and basically told me, but I didn't listen to her damn half-riddles."

Sir Ned blinked as he processed but realized seconds after Joneya that indeed the merwoman had warned them. "That's where we start." He moved over and grabbed a pen and paper. "We write down verbatim what was said, and then we start to unravel it."

Joneya started to object that she wasn't about to sit still instead of going out to look for Abaris, but she knew it was ridiculous. He wasn't in this world anymore. The merwoman and the magic doorway convinced her of that. It was possibly an elaborate trick, but the searching guards and the centaurians would figure it out if that were the case. No, she needed to work through this tangled puzzle if she wanted her best friend and lover back.

"Yup. From when we came into sight of the water then." Sir Ned began to write.

# Chapter 7 - Puzzles and Riddles

The days whirled for Joneya as she tried to solve the kidnapping from both sides of the gate - the mortal world and the land of the fae. Mystery and deceit were plentiful on both sides, but at least she also received respect on both sides. She had never been anything but true to her words and self; that was respected far more than anyone gave credit for.

Meanwhile, although Joneya could keep the public whispers at bay with discussions of a business trip, the kids were not impressed. Joneya and the staff didn't try to lie, they just varied the level of truth they gave the children. The youngest heard a greater focus on "bad people" keeping Daddy away, and the older children learned a lot about political negotiations. They all learned more about the power of perception and how perception leads to strength and power. Not one of them argued when they were informed they were staying within the small radius of the house with many more guards or they would be alongside their mother and many guards. While Joneya assured them that they weren't a target of random kidnappers, they all worried a little about political kidnappers. Joneya worried a lot actually, and her nights held very little sleep. She alternated between drinking espresso and peppermint tea. Both had attributes to keep her alert, but she absolutely preferred the taste of espresso. Peppermint tea always reminded her of being sick, probably because mint often soothes an upset belly.

The party planning continued and Joneya now had extra incentive to dig out all the little undercurrents and bribery. Not surprisingly, there were plenty of bribes regarding one person's gambling debts and another's infidelity, and another's proclivity to wear pink thongs which he did not want his spouse to know about. Joneya also found a very well run, albeit underground, brothel. The madam had quite a scare when The Hand and Lady Joneya showed up. A lot of hustling and whispering was heard all around as the madam tried to find an appropriate room to meet in. Joneya pulled aside a young woman and complimented her on her powder blue, frilly dress. Soon they were chatting at ease and then Joneya announced that they would use this lass's room for a talk. She paid the young lady a stipend for rent of her room for three hours (they were there less than one) and asked if she could have some hot tea and coffee delivered.

By the time they had left the brothel, the madam was an official business paying taxes to the kingdom, making sure her employees received regular health screenings (she already did this), and had no more worries of calling the police if a customer became too rough. They agreed to check on the actual ordinances for how large the sign out front could be, and now that it was to be in the open, that it would be an innuendo appropriate for children to read, but clear enough for potential clients.

At the same time, these mundane dramas were being unearthed, Joneya was finding more and more disgruntlement in the fae lands. Now, it should be noted that fae lands does not just mean the land of the fae, but a land of magical beings. It did not take long before there was a meeting with the merfolk to learn that they were upset with the endless ships and boats upon their waters and the dangers those same boats caused the merfolk, not to mention the pollution from all those ships. Further, when the crab waters had been extended further out in the ocean, the boats now traveled dangerously close to where the merfolk lived and spent most of their time. They demanded a sanctuary of safe space in the waters. There was, of course, the slight issue of some of it being in International Waters and beyond Joneya's control, but they reached an agreement of what laws could be regulated and enforced with a glamour to provide the rest of the deterrent.

The dryads took this time to point out that they had been edged out of most of the councils and replaced with silly nymphs. The nymphs, unsurprisingly, were upset to be thought of as just frolicking, silly creatures, and pulled forth their entire history for Joneya to read. Luckily, she already knew the highlights, positive and negative, and pacified the nymphs by comparing their history to that of the dryads, the fae, and the busquarae. At which point she could readdress the issue of the dryads having lost council spots (the nymphs hadn't actually gained any large number) and promised to research that issue further.

At 10pm this Wednesday evening, Joneya sat at her desk in her library. Her eldest son, Larseth, was curled up on the couch reading. The younger three had piled blankets and pillows over in a corner and were watching some tv series about a fictional royal family that was currently missing the royal pet monkey.

A knock at the hallway door and simultaneously, a ring sent up from the cottage broke Joneya's concentration. The ring meant that someone had arrived at the cottage and was letting her know that they had arrived. She would wait for the next signal to see whether they expected an audience with her as soon as possible, or were willing to wait for her convenience.

The guard at the door looked through the newly installed peephole, and his eyebrows rose as he stepped back. "M'Lady."

"Yeah?" Joneya asked without looking up, then registering his tone, she looked up, eyebrow cocked.

"M'Lady, I don't know who she is, but she's important."

Joneya flicked the screen to toggle the view to the hallway camera. Then she glided to the door and immediately opened it. "Come in, Your Majesty, Arichel." Turning to the guard, Joneya added, "You're right. She is important. Let me introduce you to one of the most powerful women in the universe, Queen Arichel of Aegnya, and the biggest badass I know."

"Have we actually met, Queen Joneya?" asked the woman with the long, straight brown hair in the tight black leather pants, dark green velvet vest, and small silver tiara.

"There isn't a need to be in the same room as you, to know who you are," laughed Joneya. "Even the poor lad here knew you were important. Come in, tea? Coffee?"

"Whiskey?" smiled Arichel with the same lifted eyebrow.

"Oh yeah." Joneya moved to the side table and grabbed two large glasses. "Ice?" Seeing Arichel shake her head, Joneya poured the red gold liquid into the glasses, three quarters full. The crystal sparkled in the light, the alcohol absorbed it and burned with an internal flame. If there was an alcohol that could represent either woman, it would be whiskey.

Joneya and Arichel moved to the couch together. Immediately, they were at ease together like two old souls reunited.

"Shit's gotten real for you, hasn't it?" began Arichel with a sympathetic half smile.

Joneya snorted, "Yeah, that's one way of putting it. Worse, I feel like I'm playing catch up to a race I didn't know I was in, in the other realm, and I still have all the responsibilities here. And the fact that he's missing is just fucking bullshit. He's my rock, my best friend, my almost-everything."

"I know." Arichel completely understood. She really did. She was literally the glue that held two parallel worlds together, a royal in one and a common person's role in the other, but if she failed to meet her responsibilities, both worlds would fail. Like Joneya, she had a great support system in her court, unlike Joneya, she and her court had lived and partnered together for centuries, but the emotional ties between a husband and wife, between partners, between lovers is the same through the ages. "So let's figure this out in both realms. I hold the worlds stable, but my presence does nothing to hold the people accountable. Just like your presence holds the magic in balance, but does nothing to control who wields it."

"Yeah." Joneya sipped her whiskey. "Do you know where my husband is? Or, who is holding him?"

"No. I've heard some rumbles, but I don't know. Jarrandon is good at finding out information. I'll have him look into it." Arichel chewed her lip for a moment., "I don't want to make it sound like I think he's unimportant, but I don't think your husband was taken as a power player. I think he was used as a piece to affect you."

Joneya nodded and sighed, "I agree. He's too new to this. They, whoever the fuck 'they' are, took him to get to me."

"Yeah, but I'm not sure if it's an attack directed at you or if it's to distract you." Arichel sipped some more whiskey and then stood up to refill her glass. She brought the bottle back and set it on the low table beside them. "I think many of the fae are upset more with your family generally than you particularly."

"That's true. Some feel I shirked my duties by running away, but most know that I was still involved. I just wasn't here. But my mother made some enemies."

"She did. So this could be a kidnapping as an act of war, or it may be to distract you from something else. That's what I need to find out. But I would also like us to be friends. I have been meaning to connect with you and just...hadn't yet. Better late than never, right?"

"Absolutely!" Joneya smiled, "I completely understand the list of things to do is far longer than the hours in a day. No worries there."

"So what is your advice, Arichel? How do I find out if this is an act of war or distraction?"

"Like I said, I'll research my side of the mist and see what we can find. If it's a declaration of war, that will be loud and clear. So right now, let's talk about your side. MacKerrit said there's a party at your sister's right off. Is that important?"

Joneya's eyebrows jumped, "You know MacKerrit?"

"Oh yes, we go back a long ways. I often don't agree with his political choices, but his heart is in the right place."

"No, I tend to oppose bombing to put my point across, but I do credit him that there are almost never lives lost or even direct injuries sustained. He's always been honest and direct with me."

"He's a good guy, though he sometimes wears the villain's cloak."

Joneya snorted again and sipped more whiskey. "That's the most apt description I have ever heard."

Arichel laughed out loud too, an easy, comfortable laugh from deep in her throat.

"So what is your advice, Arichel? How do I find out if this is an act of war or distraction?"

"Like I said, I'll research my side of the mist and see what we can find. If it's a declaration of war, that will be loud and clear. So right now, let's talk about your side's details. The party at your sister's is right off. Is that important?"

"Ok, so there are a few things happening here, which may or may not have the influence of the fae, or otherworlders as the locals call them. There are some people, generally servants, going missing. It seems like that may be more a black market thing in that they are falling into debt and then disappearing, but my gut says there is something more there."

"Always follow your gut," interrupted Arichel.

"Right," Joneya gave a quick smile. "So I think there is an otherworld connection to the missing people, but I don't know what. MacKerrit was talking about is the big party held at the palace. I'll organize it," seeing Arichel's lifted eyebrow, Joneya explained, "I give my sister credit, there are some things that she knows are more my wheelhouse. She knows that I know the underside of society, that which she shouldn't even know exists, or that she should be jailing. We both know the world doesn't go round without that aspect of society, too. So I am the liaison between the classes, between the proper and legal versus the not-spoken about. The Solstice Celebration is a time when all those barriers can be dropped and everyone is welcome in my house or, in this case, our houses. The celebration is easiest held at Castle Draug for the greater space. Given recent events, I am even more happy to host it there rather than here."

"Ok," agreed Arichel, "that makes sense."

"So tomorrow, I really need to go to Castle Draug to finish the plans there. That's what I was working on here, when you arrived."

"I see. How many of your people can cross the barrier between this realm and the Fae realms?"

"I really don't have a number, and I don't think some are even aware they do it, but they assume it was a dream. The old blood runs strong and many of these families are Old Blood."

"Interesting." Arichel tapped her thumbnail against her teeth in thought. "Hmm, that makes it a little harder to track. It would be nice to narrow the focus some."

"Yeah, tell me about it." Joneya sipped more whiskey, letting it roll over her tongue before letting it burn down her throat.

"We'll set up a test at this party of yours." Arichel began thinking out loud.

Joneya lifted an eyebrow again but stayed quiet, waiting to hear more.

"We'll build something with wards. We'll see who can sense them, who avoids them, and who walks through them. Don't worry, nothing bad, just a feeling."

Joneya nodded, "Then, we have a somewhat accurate tri-sorted list. I like it."Joneya smiled, "A labyrinth."

"Hmm," Arichel pondered. "It would make sense, and it's the fun sort of thing that people like to play with. And maybe a couple other wards around the grounds, some that attract and some that repel, just to observe your guests around them."

"Uhhuh, so we'll have the traditional music, dancing, bonfires, some speeches, lots of food of course. We had been toying with doing a masquerade aspect to it, but given recent events, that is off the table. We will have some contests and prizes for the locals, it's their chance for fame."

"What sort of contests?"

"Hmm, the usual, some crafts, some pickles and pies, but most of all, the wine contests. And along with those, the brandy contests."

"You know how to throw a party!" Arichel raised her glass and Joneya clinked hers back.

# Chapter 8 - Setting Up

Arichel was no stranger to working many facets but even she marveled at how Joneya moved through the day with everyone knowing her, sharing with her, and constantly trading favors - usually information - with her. More importantly, everyone respected her, but was comfortable around her. Her phone never stopped buzzing and cryptic notes arrived all the time. Several times, Arichel watched her carry a bag or a folder from one meeting to another, never opening it, and passing it off at a later meeting. It was easy to quickly realize why they all respected her; she held a key to them all. She also, Arichel marveled, brooked no nonsense and called out several people as they tried to bullshit her. She was uncanny at knowing who was around her all the time. Arichel asked her about this, thinking she must have some sort of magic in use, a net of awareness or something. But Joneya said no, she just kept her guard up and could usually feel when people were in proximity. Some people had a stronger feeling than others. Usually she just had awareness.

The only one, who took no nonsense from Joneya, was the one who forced her to stop, sit down, and eat. The Mistress of the Kitchens took one look and shooed her over to a table, while beckoning a lass over with two bowls of soup. Shortly after, they were served warm crusty bread and with what Arichel imagined was fresh butter.

"Oh my gods, this is good!" said Arichel between spoonfuls.

"You have no idea!" answered Joneya with a laugh. "This soup is the 'kitchen leftovers' soup, as they call it. All the little bits and pieces leftover from whatever they are making, tossed in a pot and left to simmer. I'm quite sure she tosses in some spices and herbs, too. But it's not really "made". If that makes sense. Wait until you try something that she actually cares about."

"Seriously?"

"Oh yeah." Joneya laughed. "She kept me fed my whole life growing up here, you have no idea. The bread is always good. It's made in a brick oven and there's nothing like it."

"Fresh bread and butter are heavenly," agreed Arichel. "My husband would fight anyone for this." After a few more bites, Arichel suggested, "After this, let's figure out where to lay out the labyrinth and the photo ops to net everyone through."

"Net?"

"Well, it's like a net. Anything too small to be an issue passes through like a little fish. But our prey gets stuck long enough for us to capture them. Or, at least, their information." Arichel laughed, "This is the only kind of fishing I enjoy."

As they finished, Joneya said, "I don't know if you caught it, but there were references to a lot of bribery today and people not paying up on their debts. Money seems to be a big issue right now. Almost more so than the information on each other, or special skill sets that are usually in demand. Even more than smuggling, and that has always been an issue here at the castle."

"Smuggling? Really?"

"Sure, easy to avoid customs if it's a regal gift. No one checks the baggage of ambassadors. Many oddities are favored by the royals... Super easy. In and out. Besides, who's going to call the cops on someone from the castle and which cop wants to end their career early, opening an investigation?"

Arichel chewed the inside of her lip, "True."

"Actually, it might bear looking into. It's always been more or less accepted, but maybe some of the banned objects are coming through again."

"I know I'm going to regret asking, but 'banned objects'?"

"Some things I won't tolerate coming through these gates. Anything harming children, slavery of any kind, and hard drugs."

"That's admirable, in a twisted sort of way."

"Not really. Everything is traded, bought and sold, all the time. I'm a realist. I just have morals. It seems to work out ok."

"What about the totes and envelopes you transported but didn't look in? How do you know those meet your standards?"

"I guess I don't." Joneya chuckled darkly. "But, if I find out they don't meet my standards, the participants might be found dead. Or, more likely, with no one to work with anymore. I would just announce that I don't approve of them, and others distance themselves, too."

"I see," Arichel said thoughtfully. "You guard what comes through the gate."

"I guess that's one way of looking at it. Some days it's easy, some days it's messy, but never have I had a monster come through the door and take my family."

"Do we know which gate yet?" asked Arichel. "Because I think I missed that."

"Nope," answered Joneya, "but I think we can rule out the mortal world. So now we need to be checking my other gates."

"Well yeah," agreed Arichel, "but I haven't felt a single person travel through a Gate here."

"Really?" asked Joneya, surprised. "There have been a few travelers through the day that I know of. But why wouldn't you feel it?"

"Do you have wards up?"

"I don't, but maybe there are. ..." Joneya chewed the inside of her lip in thought. "Let's take a walk over there."

"There?"

"Yeah, there's one here in the gardens right near the labyrinth."

"You're kidding me."

"No, I thought you saw it when we were out there."

"Saw it? You mark it?" Arichel asked.

"Hells no. But the shimmer is there if you know where to look," Joneya chuckled as she answered.

"Don't you protect people from it?"

"What do you mean? Like from wandering through it?" Joneya was a bit incredulous.

"Sure. But I meant, from the gate opening and slicing someone right open. It happens, you know." Arichel was so confused and that confusion came through her tone.

"Apparently, my gates differ from yours. These are always open, but most people can't pass to another realm. It happens to be a real gate, so they just walk through and stay on the path right here."

"What?!"

Yeah, it's just there. But almost no one goes through it, in a magical way."

"How, I mean- How is that even possible?" Arichel seldom stuttered.

As they spoke, Joneya and Arichel had walked to where they had set up the labyrinth before. Joneya led them over to the side, as if they were looking at the flowers by the path. She nodded forward. "Can you see it?" asked Joneya. "Or, feel it?"

"I can't feel it at all, not even a little hum." Arichel looked around and tried to see any sign, any wavering of light to show the edge. "I can't even see the slightest hint."

Joneya nodded ahead, and they began to walk down the dark, blood red bricks which quickly turned to old, gray flagstones, softened with age. A tall, iron arch opened the hawthorn hedge between the open lawns and the rose garden.

"Iron? You've got to be kidding me!" Arichel stood still in disbelief.

"One of the oldest keys that there are." Joneya grinned in amusement

"True, it does work for some things." Arichel chuckled, too.

Then in a serious tone again, Joneya said, "But maybe not enough. Iron may hinder some of the fae, but not greed."

"What happens if I walk through?" asked Arichel

"Since you can't feel it, I don't know." Joneya paused, "Hold my hand, let's see."

"You are a badass. You have no idea what will happen, but you want to just waltz through."

"You have a better idea?"asked Joneya with a raised eyebrow.

Arichel laughed and looped her arm through Joneya's. "Let's continue our walk, then, yeah?"

Together, they walked through. And it was completely anticlimactic. Nothing happened except the goosebumps that raised on Joneya's arms."

"OK, so you're pulling my leg," Arichel chuckled. "Or, you don't trust me. That would make sense, too."

Joneya laughed now. "Hardly. You couldn't feel that at all?"

Arichel raised an eyebrow. "Feel it?"

Joneya slipped her arm from Arichel's. Then she walked through the gate, back the way they had come. She flickered and disappeared.

A moment later, Joneya reappeared, popping out of the air towards Arichel.

"Fuck me," breathed Arichel. "I saw the barest flicker of a waver. But I felt nothing. Nothing at all."

"So now what? What does this show us? Maybe you need to be a mortal from here? To feel it and see it?"

"No, you're not exactly mortal yourself. Demi-mortal maybe, but you said most mortals don't see it."

"So...why?"

Arichel laughed again, "because you're the keeper of the gate. Does your sister see it?"

Joneya grinned a sickly grin. "I've never asked her, but I doubt it."

"Who else can see it? Or use it?"

"A few, but I've never known a pattern except the Old Blood."

"Everyone who can see it, derives from the Old Blood?"

"As far as I know."

"That must be significant."

"Yes, and no. These are all my people, regardless of when their families settled."

"Right." Arichel chewed her lip thinking. "Ok, so Old Blood matters to see or maybe use the Old Magic, but...do many people participate in the rites you lead?"

"Sure, but most do it in a Hallmark way."

"Hallmark?"

"Sorry, mortal term. Hallmark is a company famous for selling cards. The gist of the term is that they commercialized Christmas and it no longer is the magical or religious occasion it was before."

"Hmm, so most people participate for fun, but not the meaning?"

"Exactly."

"Yeah, I think that happens everywhere."

"Queen Joneya!" The shout came from a distance, but the urgency in the stableboy's voice was clear. Joneya spun, quickly seeing the out of breath lad, running to her. She hurried towards him, Arichel in step with her.

"M'Lady, we need you, please. Please come quick!" Joneya could feel as much as see the shaky fear in him.

"Show me." Joneya was calm, but wasted no time as they walked very quickly back the way the lad had come. She would not run, nothing induced a panic like a running queen.

Within minutes they were stepping into the Royal Stables, filled with a light dust and the smell of sweet grain and fresh hay. Sawdust had recently been spread in the stalls and added a clean scent to the air. Sunlight streamed through windows, dust motes dancing in the light, and it was the most peaceful place to be, surrounded by quiet horse's movements. Until she smelled it. Joneya stopped short just a moment before Arichel. Marring the perfect place was the metallic scent of fresh blood. Pausing only a moment, as she stretched out her awareness, Joneya walked forward again.

Off to the left side, behind the short hall lined with grain bins, there was an iron gate. Arichel hissed, "The scent is stronger here, but I can't see it."

"I can." Joneya breathed slowly and calmly, taking in every detail she could see, or smell, or hear.

"M'Lady, we-we moved out the younger boys, not sure who might be able to see it or not. Not everyone can see through that gate, you know. But some of us can, and those younger boys don't need a nightmare."

Joneya loosed the breath she didn't know she was holding while he spoke. "No, you did well. Evan? Is that your name, lad?" He bobbed his head quick in response. "No Evan, you did well. They needn't see this. Do you know," Joneya paused for a moment and then continued, "Do you know if any of them could smell it?"

"I-I'm not sure."

"No, that's alright." Joneya stepped forward then. Could you find me a bucket and a sack or a grain bag or something like that? Also, send a message to one of my guards or Sir Ned, to come fetch this."

"Yes, M'Lady." He bowed his head quickly and turned away.

"Evan?" Arichel called out as he walked away.

"Yes, m'lady?"

"How many of you can see through this gate?"

"Oh, I, um, I'm not sure, m'lady. Not that many of us, I think. A few say they can, but I think they are just pretending, most of them. Only two of us, that I know, now that Nate left." Evan gave a brief nod of his head and turned again to leave.

"Hmm. Interesting."Arichel was chewing her lip again. Once they were alone, she asked, "What is it? What is the blood from? I can't see through this gate either."

Joneya had stepped right to the edge of the gate and was looking closely. She was looking for any clues she might have missed, but more, she was looking for a trap of some sort. She turned her head a little, while still keeping eyes on the gate.

"It's a dead white rabbit, slit neck, hung over a black top hat. It is designed to look like a magician's props, like an entertainment magician. The rabbit is dripping into the hat. I don't see any notes or symbols drawn or painted. I don't hear anything extra. I can't see any traps, but I'm not going to cross, just in case."

"Badass and smart," smiled Arichel. "Not sure I would wait."

# Chapter 9 - The Trouble with Gates

"I'll handle it. Ok? Just let me figure it out. OK? Just let me handle it." Joneya hit disconnect on the phone. "Fuck!" she said and threw the phone across the room. Cameras and reporters were everywhere. People were calling her from everywhere. She ignored them all. Imagine all we can learn by listening here, people. Stop fucking talking. Sir Ned didn't say a word and even her sister, Francesca, didn't say anything for a moment.

Joneya rubbed her middle fingers against her temples and closed her eyes. The headache that had just been a minor irritation in the morning was now a cyclone of stress reaction. She opened her eyes when the scent of coffee teased her nose. Sir Ned was setting a steaming mug in front of her, just as Arichel slid a glass of amber liquid over. Francesca lit a cigarette-her sign of stress was just as visible as Joneya rubbing her temples.

"I'll take care of it, ok?" sighed Joneya to Francesca. She tossed back the whiskey in one burning gulp. She picked up the mug and clasped it in both hands against her lips, and breathed in deeply through her nose. Joneya imagined the acrid cigarette smell was instead the pipe tobacco her uncle had smoked. She couldn't remember the brand, but she could still picture the packaging from thirty years ago. The ivory package with the blue ship's logo. That smell calmed her, even if it was just in her memories.

"Alright, the two are connected, obviously." Joneya began speaking calmly then, holding the mug just in front of her face, absorbing the heat and waiting for it to cool enough to sip. "First, Francesca and I will publicly announce that we are saddened that our annual event has been marred by senseless acts of mischief. We don't need to go into details, and it covers both. Solidarity in this is key."

Francesca nodded her agreement. "We should say something more, that it saddens us more that such events require us to be more...guarded - we'll think of a better word - to protect our innocent children. Anytime children are threatened, no one questions extra security, and it raises the general population's ire."

"Ok, that's smart," Joneya nodded. Her sister was good at politics. Create the statement and I'll join you for the delivery. Short and sweet, only you need to talk since this is your home-"

"It's our home," Francesca interrupted.

"Not really, no. You talk and I stand beside you. And you use the pronoun 'we'. I nod and look supportive." Joneya looked at her Hand, "Sir Ned?"

He looked up from his notes. "We'll be ready. I suppose you want to do it outside? Inside would be safer." He dipped his head when she nodded. "I thought so. I'll find a location. Also, extra guards are already on duty and others are coming on extra shifts, many in plainclothes, formal clothes, I suppose, for the event. No one from the royal family, nor you, Queen Arichel, is ever out of sight of a guard."

"Yeah," sighed Joneya. She had been expecting that. "We'll be armed, too." Hearing Francesca's intake of breath, she added, "Yes, even you. Just in case. The magician's rabbit hanging upside down, dripping blood, is pretty clearly a threat. Let's not forget your childhood callsign."

"No one knew that!"

Joneya snorted. "You didn't grow out of 'The White Rabbit' when you stopped reading Alice in Wonderland. They changed it once it was compromised."

"But, I, but-" Francesca looked at Sir Ned, who nodded.

"'Tis true, lass," he said.

"Well, shit."

"Yeah," Joneya laughed softly. "That sums it up."

Francesca sat down hard on the edge of the couch. "I didn't realize it was me. I thought it was just a magician's rabbit, and you're the wielder of magic here. So I thought it was directed at you."

Joneya just raised an eyebrow at her sister and drank her coffee, waiting for her to understand. Her phone buzzed across the room.

"Oh, double shit!" Now, Francesca was rubbing her temples, too. "It was directed at you, but I'm still the damn rabbit. Fuck!"

"Yeah." Joneya stood up and handed out the glasses that Arichel had just poured. "Abracafuckingdabra, sis."

True to her old call sign, Queen Francesca was late to the press release. But no one was surprised. There had been a brief argument when Francesca had suggested getting a magician for children's entertainment "to show them that magic isn't scary."

Joneya blinked at her for a moment, weighing her thoughts before asking, "Are you serious?"

"Of course! We don't want them to fear magicians because of these crude pranks."

Joneya pinched the bridge of her nose. "That's a terrible idea." She opened her eyes and looked straight at Francesca. "No. We're not doing that."

"But-"

"No. We're not doing that. We don't need to."

"But-"

"No." The quiet voice was absolutely final and Francesca didn't broach the argument again. Joneya sighed then. "The ones who do believe in magic know the difference between the parlor tricks like you are talking about and the Auld Magic. Anyone who doesn't understand will just think it's a petty crime in poor taste. We do the press release and we find out who is behind these messages. That's it."

"Ok."

Arichel met Joneya's eyes, and Joneya could see the respect. "I'm going to leave for a little while. I want to check some information back home. But I would like to be back tonight for the party."

Joneya nodded. Francesca spoke with many flowery phrases and thanked Arichel for coming and, of course, she was welcome back tonight. Francesca followed Arichel out of the room, still gushing her chipper words.

Joneya sighed. "Sir Ned?"

"Yes M'Lady. So, no fingerprints at the rabbit scene beyond the stableboys and such. No helpful shoe prints, etc. It seems to be a common pet rabbit, easily available and often sold at a variety of stores. The same for the top hat. Quite common and untraceable."

"A dead end then, just the message."

"So it seems. Likewise, the noose-are you certain we shouldn't tell your sister?" Seeing Joneya's curt nod, Sir Ned continued, "The noose in your sister's quarters, also divulged nothing helpful at the scene except the cord itself."

Joneya looked up questioningly, "Yeah?"

"The cord is a different...texture, than anything I have felt before. Arichel asked me to tell you that she thought it felt familiar. We agreed to cut a sample off for her to bring back to her home city and check around. She was, um, concerned, that you might feel slighted that we didn't ask you first."

Joneya waved her hand. "I trust you to lead the investigation as you feel fit. You know that."

Sir Ned nodded. "I thought so, M'Lady."

"Nor have we forgotten that a passing rabbit is an omen of nature and fertility." Joneya snorted then, "Fertility, yeah." Even Sir Ned cracked a smile. "So, the nature part might be to send the message that the Fae, i.e. nature, are breaking with us. It might have nothing at all to do with magic."

Sir Ned nodded, looking seriously annoyed. "I didn't even realize-I should have seen that. I'm sorry, M'Lady-"

"Hush. None of us are perfect."

Sir Ned dipped his head, "But if we consider this meaning, then we need to find out who is represented by the hat."

"Who was The MadHatter, Sir Ned?"

"Your father. So I don't think that is it."

Arichel rubbed her temples again. "Maybe my sister is right in her theory, but let's follow this, too.. Angry fae & merpeople, or discrediting magic, or some whacko. It's good to have choices, right?"

Sir Ned nodded, letting the sarcasm wash right over him and poured himself a shot of whiskey. "I would offer you one, but I know you have the wine and brandy tasting soon." He held his glass out to her in a toast, "To solving mysteries."

"To mysteries," agreed Joneya. "Alright, let's round up my sister and do this announcement. Then I am spending time with my children until I need to do last-minute whatevers for this party."

After a rousing afternoon of card games, and then a mandatory rest time of a movie, Joneya and her family dressed for the party. The children could dress less formally in tennis skirts for the girls and khaki shorts for the boys. The girls had comfy blouses, and the boys had polo shirts. They looked like they were ready for a yacht party or corporate picnic. They were each given the option of wearing a circlet upon their head in symbolism of a crown, but unsurprisingly, they declined. Instead, the boys each wore a signet ring of their choosing and a leather bracelet with old symbols carved into the leather. The girls each wore their hair braided into a simple crown with flowers woven in.

Joneya however, was not dressed so casually. She, too, wore her hair braided into a crown, but an actual tiara was nestled in and flowers and greenery woven through both. Her dress was long, tight in the bust, folded at the waist and flowing down her legs, loose and light. Her shoulders were mostly bare with stretchy black lace just clinging to the edge of her shoulder. The entire dress was a shimmering, dark green satin, but with more black lace across the bodice and accenting the skirt and edges. It was somber, yet not depressing. Also, it would be easy to run in it, should the need arise. Likewise, instead of heels as she would normally wear on this occasion, Joneya chose sandals for ease of movement. Lastly, she accentuated herself with silver, blue, and green talisman jewels. It was modest. And it was gorgeous.

Just before she left her room, Joneya lit a yellow candle for clarity and knowledge, and invoked The Morrigan:

To see the Truth,

to know the way,

I cast a spell in every way,

by the power of Three

I conjure thee,

to give thy Truth unto me.

Everyone seemed to be having a grand time at the gala. The wine tasting and then the brandy tasting were hits with the adults, just as the face painting was amazing for the little kids. Food and music were bountiful.

"This is beautiful, Joneya." Queen Francesca sidled up to her sister and spoke softly while smiling widely at everyone nearby. "I don't know how you do all of this so easily."

"I don't really do much," answered Joneya. "There are plenty of systems in place. It just has to be put in motion."

"Yeah, it's not that easy-"

"Don't think you're ssso sspesscial, Queen." The voice slithered to them, oily and grotesque. Joneya's instinct was to shiver and step away, but she kept her face still and refused to shy away. Francesca gave a muffled scream, though and jumped.

Before Francesca completely lost it, Joneya quietly spoke without turning around. She wouldn't give the satisfaction and she trusted that Sir Ned had her back. The Auld Blood was deep in his veins and he could see through any glamour. "Hmm, I must have misplaced your invitation. Please tell me where it should have found you."

The voice laughed an oily, gravely laugh. "What, no welcome for me now?"

"Well, of-"

Joneya stepped on her sister's foot and smoothly spoke as if she hadn't heard Francesca speaking. "Unlikely. We both know why. So why don't you tell me who you speak for and what the message is?"

The voice hissed in anger and then chuckled, "You do not disssssssa-point, Little One. They said you were careful, but I tend not to believe it of puny humansss."

Joneya kept her face perfectly neutral, but her thoughts spun. She couldn't place the sibilant accent, and the sound of the voice suggested a looming presence, combined with him/it calling her Little One. She decided she had made the point of not showing fear and gracefully turned to face him, nerves steeled for any sight. He spoke again as she looked at him.

"I sssspeak for mysssself, Little One. I am no messenger!" Irritation and mirth danced in his voice. However, he looked surprisingly...nor-mal.

Joneya moved her hands to clasp gently behind her back. But as she did, she caught Sir Ned's eyes and flicked her fingers as she brought them back. Sir Ned nodded and then spoke curtly into his watch. Joneya casually brushed her right hand across her eyebrow and back as if tucking a strand of hair out of her eyes and behind her ear. Then, she returned to casually clasping her hands behind her. Sir Ned would therefore bring in reinforcements, but they would watch and wait.

"My apologies, Sir?" Joneya spoke softly and calmly, noting his dressy but somewhat worn shoes, impeccable suit, and both of his hands in plain view. Meeting her gaze, he lifted a glass of brandy to his full, dark lips and took a sip. He then tossed his head ever so slightly, shaking his mid length, dark brown hair out of his eyes. As he did so, Joneya caught movement to both sides of them in her peripheral vision. She tapped her left thumb against her right hand twice. A moment later, Sir Ned rubbed his cheek with two fingers. The message relayed from behind her and received.

"You might call me, Stopus."

Joneya nodded her head, "Is that your real name?"

"What is real?" he countered.

"Fair enough." Joneya chuckled too and loosened her shoulders. It would seem that she wasn't under immediate physical threat. She knew Sir Ned had sent extra guards to her children. She just had to tease out this situation. But her sister was a problem.

"What do you mean," Francesca's voice started to raise from a whisper to a hushed shriek, "what is real?"

"Hush," Joneya was firm but not unkind. "Perhaps Stopus would be kind enough to let you go find your darling husband, while he and I speak."

Stopus inclined his head, "Yesss, that would be fine."

"Really?" whispered Francesca with astonishment.

"Uhhuh, I would suggest looking near the axe throwing. He seems to enjoy those games," suggested Joneya. And it just happens to be on the opposite side of this party.

"Ok, I mean, if you, if you don't-" apparently Francesca did have some feelings of responsibility.

"Go ahead," Joneya smiled reassuringly. "Go find him, while our new acquaintance and I speak." Francesca wasted no more time.

"Well done, Little One."

"Thanks," replied Joneya dryly. "You have a message for me? From yourself, apparently?"

"Why sssuch a russh?"

"Well, you know, I have this party I am hosting and I tend not to stay with any guests for very long. So, if we don't want to draw too much attention to you...?"

He laughed that oily, gravelly laugh again. "Point for you. We could be an excellent team, Little One." Joneya lifted an eyebrow, he continued speaking, "My friendsss would like for me to tell you sscertain thingsss and to hmmmm, to threaten you. But jusst because they want thingsss from me doessn't mean that isss what I want."

"Uhhuh."

"Yesss, you are intelligent and calm. Fearsssome. You are in a tight ssspot, I think, but not because of your errorss. I can help you."

"And you would help me because?"

"I would rather have you with me, than againsst me, Little One."

"That's comforting," Joneya scoffed. "You will help me as long as it benefits you. What about when it doesn't?"

"Then we ssee don't we?" He shook his hair out of his eyes again and Joneya noted that the two other figures moved further away. "I have heard many thingsss about you, how weak you are, and ssssilly, but you don't match that." He narrowed his eyes, "When did you come back near thessse portalss?"

Joneya narrowed her eyes, "Assuming your portals are the same as my gates," he nodded impatiently, "then quite recently. I was quite distant from them for a long time."

He nodded, in his own thoughts. "Yessss, I thought asss much. Who wasss sssshe?"

Without hesitation, Joneya replied, "My mother."

"Ahh, yesss." He smiled then, his teeth alarmingly bright and slightly feral. "You are in danger, dessspite the forces of magic that ssssswirl around you, Little One."

"I have a huge amount of backup. You aren't going to hurt me, but if you do, a world of shit is going to rain down on you. And then another world, and another world. Your choice." Joneya wasn't bragging and her voice stayed even and calm. That's what made it deadly serious. She had no doubt.

Stopus laughed outright. "Oh yessss, Little One, I like you and your confidensssce."

Joneya raised an eyebrow again.

He clarified, "I will make you a promisssse, which you will come to undersstand is a grand thing for me to make, essspesssscially ssince I have jusst met you."

# Chapter 10 – New Friends

S topus clarified, "I will make you a promisssse, which you will come to undersssstand is a grand thing for me to make, es- ssspesssscially ssssince I have jusst met you."

"Oh, yeah?"

"Indeed, Little One. I will join you on your hunt. I will watch your back, even. And if I decide to break my fidelity to you, I will honessstly tell you."

Joneya bit the inside of her lip. Her gut said that he spoke the absolute truth. He might be the most honest, dishonest person she had met. She wasn't sure that he was a person, but he was telling her the truth. She wanted all the help she could have for her hunt for Abaris. "Alright then. We are allies until we decide not to be, and we are forthcoming if we reach that point."

"Yessss, Little One." They shook hands then, despite the intense danger that Joneya put herself in by doing that. She also dropped the lightest net she could over his left shoe. She was sure he would feel it if she dropped it on him, but maybe not his belongings.

"I have a question then, in good faith, if you will."

"Go ahead, Little One, asssk me."

"What are you?"

He laughed again softly, gravely but no longer oily, "I come from a world you do not know. I am like a guivre."

"I see." It fit, Joneya immediately decided, a serpentine-like creature similar to a dragon. "Please, help yourself to food and drink if there is anything that you or your comrades would find enjoyable."

"Comradesss," His mouth quirked in another smile, "Yesss, Little One, in our human form we do enjoy sssome of your foodssss and drinksss. And yesss, we will ressspect your boundaries and ssstay outside," he paused, "for now."

The gala continued late into the evening with no further adventures. Joneya watched her unexpected guests mingle flawlessly with the mortals. A few ladies came up to her to ask her about the sexy frenchmen who were visiting. Joneya answered rather vaguely. Several times, Stopus caught her eye and raised his glass in greeting.

Before taking his leave, Stopus came to Joneya and quietly said, "I ssshoud very much like to ssspeak to you tomorrow."

"I can be at your disposal to speak. Where would you like to meet?"

"I undersstand there isss a cottage at your property which is generally conssidered to be neutral territory?"

"It is. But I make no promises as to who will be there."

"Undersstood." He stepped back then and gravely bowed to her.

Joneya dipped her head, "Tomorrow then."

The day following the gala tended to start late for most people, perhaps in part from the copious brandy and beer of the night before. However, neither Castle Draug's servants nor Joneya started late. Therefore, neither did Sir Ned (if he even knew how) nor the guards.

Just after dawn, they were out on the lawns cleaning. Joneya was out checking wards and resetting her nets on the gates to be aware of when they were passed through. Generally, she was checking but not expecting anything amiss, since she had been here late the night before. Joneya checked in with the key leaders of the Castle staff and then left them to run their own departments. They knew what needed to be accomplished to put the property back to rights and to continue their daily life. Joneya returned to House Isilme before long and before her children had awakened.

Two centaurians in human form met her at the driveway and they slowly walked to The Cottage. Like her regular guards who accompanied her, they were used to any manner of strange beings coming and going from the cottage through the day.

Despite that, as the wind blew from woods, one centaurian made a very whicker-like sound of concern and rubbed at his nose.

"Marshall," hissed the other, "get ahold of yourself."

"Sorry, that scent-"

"Be alert, but remember where you are and who you are."

"Yes, sorry." He visibly straightened, but his eyes continued to dart around.

Joneya lifted an eyebrow questioningly. The calmer centaurian answered, "It is an odd scent, a dry sort of musk. But we should have been prepared for oddness." He sent a glare to the younger centaurian who blushed fiercely.

"Does it perhaps smell like an enormous snake?" asked Joneya quietly.

Both centaurians wrinkled their forehead while breathing deeply. "Yeah," nodded the elder, "it does."

Sitting by the fire, they spoke as tension filled the room. Joneya was in a blue flowing shirt over jeans, her sandals tossed beside her. Stopus was in a white T-shirt stretched over a muscled chest with black jeans and shiny black boots.

"Your problem isss a ssmart criminal who issss an old fae."

"Hmm," Joneya was noncommittal, but it made sense.

"You are ssmart enough to ssee it to be true." He continued to speak calmly and slowly in that suave sibilant voice. "You know that it isss ssomeone who can travel through the gatesss. But he isss ssmart or he wouldn't trick you. He wouldn't esscape your eyesss."

"Who is it?" Joneya didn't really expect a straight answer but it was worth a shot.

Stopus laughed low, and flashed a bright grin. "No, my queen, you have to earn that."

"I'm your queen, but you won't tell me the name?" she raised an eyebrow.

"No, it'sss not how I roll. You musst earn it."

"So I have earned the title, but not the truth."

He blinked slowly. She could have sworn an inner eyelid blinked sideways. "Yesss, ssimplisstically."

Joneya poured herself a mug of dark, spicy tea and offered him some. "Ok. What do I need to do?"

He shook his head at the tea. "I knew you were not like your mother." He spoke softly, with his head tilted to the side.

Joneya shrugged, "Err, no. Not in many ways at all."

He laughed then. It sounded like paper sliding against paper, but it was full of mirth.

"You have lossst your powers. ...not all of them, but you are but a ssshadow of what you ssshould be."

Joneya was taken aback. She had only seen herself as powerful, or holding herself back in the shadows. Never had she felt that her powers had waned.

"You are confused. I sssuspected asss much when we sspoke the other day, but that was not the time to discuss it." Stopus spoke gently and seemed to be choosing his words with care. "You have been trained to care, but you have been caring too much. It takesss the lifeforssss from you. My queen, you are one of the mosst powerful creaturesss on the planet right now, but that you can't sseize that full power until you sstart being yoursself."

Joneya blinked quickly, but she realized it felt right. His words rang with surety and truth. She looked at him and didn't say a word, but slowly sipped her tea.

He stared right back, "You feel the truth, I ssee that. Let it ssit for a moment. For a while. But not too long."

Joneya chewed the inside of her lip, but nodded. "Ok. What else will you tell me?"

"Good," he nodded. "I hoped you would believe or at least move forward asss if you believe." Seeing Joneya flash a rueful smile and he continued. "You have three problems, but luckily, they are interconnected. First, your power has never been fully birthed. We can work on that. Sssecond, you have become the gate through which vampiresss are couriering drugsss through, but it'sss not the vampsss that need you to stop, but the one behind them. Third, your lover hasss been taken, and you want him back."

"Want him back," she repeated, "Well, yes, I want him back!"

"Of courssss you do, but not all might feel the same in your shoesss."

"I-" she paused and nodded, "ok, I see that. I do want him back, but I don't want drugs smuggled through my land either. They're connected, you said?"

"Yesss, but we musst needsss to birth your power fully too, or elssss we'll just be back in a similar situation again."

"How do we do that?"

"I needsss some time to figure that out for you." He chuckled that dry paper on paper laugh again. "It's not like I wave a magic wand."

# Chapter 11 – Confirming our Alliances

Joneya was re-energized in the next few days. Her children had her almost-undivided attention through parts of the day; she was up early and late working. Joneya got caught back up on the day to day mundane running of her properties, caught up in the regular correspondence. She reached out to set up future meetings with various peoples for her public and official role, as well as her lesser known roles. Finally, she wrote out personalized notes to everyone who attended the gala at Castle Draug, as well as everyone who had sent a message that they could not attend. She then took these names and created three lists: "Completely trusted until now", "Not well known", and "Check these first!"

Sir Ned held open the door for a lad carrying in a coffee tray. Any royal house except House Isilme might have been shocked by having the High Priestess's Fist hold open the door for a mere serving lad, but not here. The lad simply nodded his thanks and then set down the tray on the side table near the library sitting area. "M'Lady, would you like me to pour?"

Joneya looked up from her papers, "If you wouldn't mind, that would surely help."

"Yes, mum." Like all the staff of House Isilme and Castle Draug, he addressed her formally first and then easily dropped into the far less formal address. Not only less formal, but like addressing an honored family member.

He carefully tapped a little natural sugar into a thick mug, then poured out strong dark coffee, topped with a heady dollop of cream. He smiled as he set the mug within reach, along with a plate with two large, soft chocolate chip cookies.

"Ah, Declan, you're spoiling me. Thank you!" laughed Joneya softly.

As the lad set another plate and mug nearby as Sir Ned slid into the chair. "Thank you, lad." Declan bobbed his head and withdrew, softly closing the heavy library door behind himself.

Sir Ned took a slow sip of coffee and contemplated the cookies. There was nothing quite so enjoyable as a thick, soft chocolate chip cookie. But he wasn't in the mood. There was nothing enjoyable about the fact that under his watch he had failed. He had failed to keep all members of House Isilme safe. Sir Ned had failed to keep the husband of the woman he considered a daughter safe. He had failed to keep safe all of the royal family under his care. He had failed.

"Stop it," chided Joneya.

"What?" asked Sir Ned, roused from his dark thoughts.

"It's not your fault any more than it's mine. We were attacked because of the actions of my mother, or maybe the inactions, but whatever." Joneya waved her hand dismissively. "Sure, we were lax about considering an assault from the other worlds, and I didn't realize how much I was missing, but neither of those are your fault. It's mine. It's my role, not yours. I'm the one who left here years ago and allowed this rift to open. It's my fault, Sir Ned."

Joneya gave him the most severe mom face she could while chastising him. Truthfully, she didn't blame him for feeling guilty; she did too. But, she needed them to actively work on solving this problem, not wallow in self guilt.

Sir Ned met her eyes and held them. He didn't say a word, but Joneya could see him thinking through what she had said, and then rallying his energies up.

Now they were ready. There would be reckoning, but first there was some setting up.

"Right," said Sir Ned, taking the cookie fuel, "what have you got?"

Joneya bit into her own cookies and took another sip of coffee. Then she set down the cookie as she slid her notebook over to Sir Ned. "Here are my three lists. I think we work on the first and last to begin with. It should be fairly easy to eliminate most of the Completely Trusted-"

"-Until now," he interrupted.

"Well, that's the rub, right? But I'm hoping they have easy alibis and cut our research down quickly." Seeing Sir Ned nod his head, she continued, "But this other list, my Check Now! list, this one can't be ignored."

"And the ones on the middle list?"

"I guess we set those aside. We have to prioritize."

"Hmm." Sir Ned had the same habit of chewing the inside of his lower lip. "Or perhaps we give that list as an assignment for the trainees. Standard background checks are something they need to practice. These names shouldn't strike any urgency, but not seem unlikely either for a 'standard check'. And any recruit worth their salt knows the swirling issues and will understand the need for checking everyone..."

"Would it be better to have them do our friends we are confident in then?"

"No, saying we're checking everyone, and then actually being seen checking everyone, are two different things."

"Uhhuh." Joneya drank more coffee. "Do what you think best then, but training practice is good. Now this third list," seeing Sir Ned nod his head, Joneya continued while sipping her coffee, "But this other list, my Check Now! list, this one can't be ignored."

"Right. Do we worry that they know we're checking into them?" asked Sir Ned.

"If they don't think we're checking them, they're idiots. And, I don't think anyone on that list is stupid." This was why Joneya didn't want to be the 'real' queen. She hated politics and just wanted to be direct all the time. "I don't like this, Sir Ned. I don't give a shit about the intrigue or the politics."

"I know, lass," he replied softly.

"I just want to help my people, live a quiet life, and nurture the magic. I want harmony and balance, not this crap."

"But here we are."

"What's that quote, 'don't mistake that because we come in peace we aren't ready for war'?" Joneya mused.

"We're ready for war, lass, if need be."

"Right. So here's the plan: trainees checking the middle list, and we'll follow up on their findings. Your most trusted people will run the checks on our friends and these flagged names." Sir Ned nodded at each point she made. "We'll confirm our allies just in case we are going to war."

Sir Ned nodded gravely again. "The Centaurians seem secure, but we'll clarify what resources they will share."

"Uhhuh. And I need to have another conversation with my Mer-friend and King Cern."

"Take Cern with you when you visit her. Show her how you have been aware of your responsibilities."

"Hmm, yeah."

"We'll have others too, but maybe I'll hold back on this. We do relatively trust her, so let's let it look like you just have regular guards and he's joining you. We both know he'll tear you away without a second's hesitation if he feels you are in imminent danger."

"Mmm. Will he? I wouldn't whisk him away from a challenge?"

"Wouldn't you if you thought he was about to be harmed?" Sir Ned lifted an eyebrow.

"Well-, damn." Joneya chuffed a laugh. "Ok, I see where you're going. Neither of us would back down from a challenge, but we wouldn't hinder the other from rising up for one either."

"A little more than that, Lass." Sir Ned laughed softly. "Your king would do almost anything to save your life and therefore both your realms. You two are the life force that brings vitality, fertility, and strength to both."

"Well, ...hmmm." There really was no argument to that. For years at Beltane and other ceremonies, they had linked their life forces together and worked their magic together so often that their energies were woven through the land together. It would be entirely different outcomes whether they chose to dissipate that energy or whether it was torn apart, whether they chose other partners or one of them were killed.

"Fine, Cern will come with me. Well, I'll ask that Cern come with me."

"Right." Knowing he was right, and that she saw it, Sir Ned just moved on with the business at hand. "Now these lists. Is there anyone from this urgent list you want to check first? Your new friend, the guivre perhaps?"

"Stopus needs to be checked because he's new. But unless his glamour is exceptionally strong, I do trust him, strangely."

"Hmm," Sir Ned tapped his lip with his thumb and then chewed another bite of cookie. After swallowing, he said, "He does have a level of calm about him, but also is completely honest that there is no real reason to trust him. That seems to make him all the more trustworthy, doesn't it? I don't think he will be surprised that we look into him."

"No, I imagine he expects it. We would do the same for anyone new approaching us and especially someone claiming to have special knowledge. I certainly wouldn't blame him, roles reversed."

"Yeah. Ok, then who?"

As expected, King Cern arrived almost immediately after Joneya had sent word that she needed him. He arrived at House Isilme in the accompaniment of a few men and women, some of whom Joneya recognised and some she didn't.

"I hope you don't mind," Cern said to Joneya with a warm smile as they met in her library, "but I brought a few of my friends."

"Of course," Joneya smiled, welcoming them all, "your friends are always welcome here. We'll shortly have rooms available. I'm afraid I don't know all of you, but we have plenty of rooms for you each to have your own space, or you may share as you like. There's no need for secrecy here. Please let me know any time if you need anything. Please, sit, have something to eat and drink." A couple of servants handed out hot and cold drinks as the guests preferred and offered small sandwiches and fruits. "The only less-than-welcoming aspects I must warn you of, and I'm sorry for this, is that our borders have a few extra guards and my children are quite closely watched. Don't take this personally. These restrictions have been in place for a couple of weeks."

Cern spoke again with a raised brow and concern heavy in his voice, "Extra guards isn't quite your style, Joneya. Is everything alright?"

"No." Joneya sank exhaustedly onto the couch and Cern was by her side immediately. "Things are rough right now. It's why I called you."

"My friends," Cern spoke softly to his entourage, "perhaps you could let my queen and I have some time alone?" The other men and women hurried out of the library and Cern wrapped Joneya in his strong arms. The smell of the forest and the mountains enveloped her. Joneya's shoulders loosened for the first time in weeks, as tension she didn't even know she had been holding leeched out. The tears came then. Quietly slipping down her face at first, Cern's thumb wiping them away and then harder until wracking sobs shook her whole body. Cern held her, his strong arms around her, pulling her whole body against his hard chest. At first he didn't say anything, but simply held her. She was like a dam that had burst and he knew the pent-up emotions had to let their force free.

Her sobs waned and then stopped, but Cern still held her. He shifted her in his arms though so her cheek pressed against his chest, his strong arm wrapping around her and holding her tight, but his other hand brushed back her hair and softly stroked her face. Tears still slipped down, but her emotions were calming. "You're going to tell me what has you in this state and we're going to find the best solution." She nodded, not yet ready to speak. "And," his gravely voice paused, "you're going to tell me why your mortal husband, whom I liked 'til now, isn't the one here by your side. Why haven't you been comforted in his arms?"

"Well, that's the problem, there."

"Where is he?"

"I don't know."

"You don't know where he's gone?"

"No, but-"

"-But not. If he has left you, we shall find him." He paused then, lifting her chin to look at him, "Unless you don't want him found."

She chuckled without mirth. "Oh, I want him, but we haven't found who took him yet."

His gravelly voice, so delicious in her ear, then swore a number of colorful oaths as he understood, and she couldn't help but smile a little. After a moment, he settled her back against the couch and handed her a cup. He grabbed his and took a drink. Then, leveling his eyes at her, Cern said, "Tell me everything. I feel strongly that our kingdom can help with this. The powers we raise are not just for growing plants, but to harness our magics to protect our people, too."

Joneya sipped her coffee and sighed. "Yeah, I hadn't really thought of it that way. I always think of myself as the caretaker, the one to gather and direct the power, not to wield it."

"Ahh, my Love, you have my entire armies at your call and together we hold more magic than any other realm. This is your birthright, this is our birthright, this is who we are."

"Yeah," Joneya took a deep breath. "Ok then. Here's what I know."

***

King Cern and Joneya spent hours in the library with different meetings of his people and hers. By afternoon, a number of other guests had arrived from Cern's court. Dinner that night was a festive affair, and for the first time since the gala, the children were entertained and having fun.

Slowly, as the conversation became more adult the children tired, and then Joneya and Mariella brought them to bed. The older three agreed to have a slumber party of movies and snacks in the larger bedroom, and Ravous couldn't be left out. A few other of Cern's guests had brought children, too. So they were content for the night together despite all the activity downstairs. Mariella was the unofficial in-room guard, and other guards were posted as usual.

Joneya returned to the guests as they moved from the dining room and to the library. A variety of alcohols and desserts, fruits, and cheeses were available and people broke off into chatting clusters and movement. Slowly people drifted off to bedrooms and soon there were only Cern, Joneya, and Daphne left.

"We should go to bed as well," Joneya said to Cern and Daphne. "There are bedrooms beside mine for each of you, or however you choose."

As they stepped through the hall, Daphne wrapped her arm in Joneya's and said, "This is not how I would imagine us growing closer, but in the future, when things have calmed down, I hope that you will come to my house for a visit, just as friends, that we may chat like this."

Joneya smiled, "I would like that very much."

Daphne continued, "You're right, what you said before, we tend to interact for our ceremonies and not much else. I, for one, would like to strengthen our friendship through the year."

"Me too," Joneya agreed. "It can only make us better."

Daphne gave Joneya's cheek a quick kiss, and they squeezed each other goodnight.

Joneya stood by her door, held open by her guards. "You are in the next room, or you could join me here for a while." The guards didn't shuffle at all, and Joneya noticed that Sir Ned had assigned older guards, ones descended from the Old Blood, and those who practiced Beltane and similar activities.

Cern inclined his head and followed her into her room. The door closed softly behind them and they were alone again. But this time did not have Joneya sobbing in his arms. The energy in the room raised the hairs on her arms.

Cern stepped close and raised her chin with his firm hand. He held her gaze and said, "I'm here to partner with you however you want. You want to talk, we talk; you want me to hold you while you cry or sleep, then I just hold you safe; if you want to mate, then we couple like we do each summer." He leaned down and brushed her lips with his. "You're my queen and I'm your king, and together we keep our kingdom strong."

"I think I forgot just how much we love each other too, you know," Joneya spoke softly and bit her lip.

"Loving each other doesn't detract from how we love our spouses, Joneya." Cern kissed her again, more firmly. "Together we are stronger." His hot lips captured hers.

Joneya's arms went up and clasped behind his neck as his large hands cupped her back and pulled her body against his. No space between them. Warmth bloomed within her as his burning lips captured her again. Joneya slid her hands under his shirt, running her hands over his chest, then along his sides, noting how his skin twitched at her touch. He was so like Abaris and yet so different.

Cern broke their kiss to pull his shirt over his head with one hand, while his other hand supported her back as he moved them towards the bed. Joneya moved her hands down, sliding her thumbs along the V and then slipping her right hand into his pants. Cern's breath hitched as she brushed her fingers along his hard erection. He tangled fingers in her hair and pulled her head back, exposing her neck. It was Joneya's turn to gasp and then moan softly as his kisses and hot breath trailed along her neck and down her cleavage. Cern released her hair as he lifted her shirt over her head and then cupped her breasts. He gently pinched and rolled her nipples as his mouth captured hers again.

Cern broke the kiss and nipped his way down Joneya's throat and to her breasts. As his tongue flicked the sensitive nipples, she gasped. His teeth nipped, and she felt herself get wetter. Her hand had been gently touching him, now grabbed with full force and began stroking hard, pulling steadily and then sliding with a firm grip back up his shaft. Cern groaned again and pushed her back, so the mattress caught the back of her legs and they dropped to the bed.

Cern and Joneya wiggled out of their clothes, desperate hands pushing and tugging against the fabric until their naked bodies were free. Hands and lips roved and burned where they touched. One of Cern's hands cupped her breast and then teased the nipple again, while his hot breath and then his tongue flicked her other nipple. His free hand slid down and his finger began to dance along her clit. She was more than ready and already drenched. Cern laughed softly as she squirmed and spread her legs wider.

Joneya enjoyed the sensations for a moment and then slid down some so she could better reach. One hand wrapped again around Cern's shaft and the other just barely reaching his balls and tugging softly. Cern threw back his head and closed his eyes.

The fire was burning brighter and heat rolled from the flames to match the inferno between their bodies. A nonexistent wind gusted through the bedroom, and it felt like the whole world paused a moment. Cern pulled back from Joneya and kissed her again, his mouth crashing into hers. Her hands slid up his ribs and to his shoulders. His knee nudged her legs wider and then he grazed against her opening. Joneya moaned and pulled against his shoulders.

"I want you in me, now," she breathed with need.

Cern teased her just a moment longer, rubbing his tip against her clit and then plunging deep inside. Joneya clenched around him and they paused a moment. Then Cern pulled back and plunged again. Faster and faster they moved their hips together, pushing against each other, frantic to touch every nerve. Joneya's fingers dug into his shoulders, and Cern flung his head back as he plunged deeper than before. Joneya cried out as her orgasm met his, clenching and pumping together.

Cern collapsed on top of Joneya, yet careful to leave her face clear. After a moment, he raised himself back up on his elbow and kissed her again, softer but just as firm.

"I can't walk yet," and they both chuckled drunkenly, "but when I can, do you want me to stay or to go to my room?"

"That's entirely up to you," Joneya smiled, content with either choice. "Stay here if you don't want to move, go there if you want to sprawl out. Either way." She rolled over to reach for the glass beside the bed and took a sip. "Either way," she handed him the glass, "have some water."

"Thank the gods!" Cern grabbed the glass and swallowed deeply before handing it back for Joneya to finish.

# Chapter 12 - Making Plans

"I feel like we are making battle plans." Joneya stated as she buttered her toast. Sir Ned met her eyes but didn't say anything.

Cern was the one who replied, "They don't have to be battle plans, but we do need to consider that."

The dining-room door opened and Stopus strode in. He nodded to Sir Ned and inclined his head to Joneya. When he saw Cern, with the rottweiler laying content at his feet, he chuckled. "Now I undersstand the energy of the night. That wasss quite a ssstorm. A good electrical sstorm can clear the air and create a fresh ssstart in the morning, don't you think?"

"Hmm," agreed Cern, eyeing Stopus. "I'm not sure that I have seen a guivre in person, so to speak, before." Turning to Joneya, he added, "You do have strange friends, my queen."

"Yeah," she said, "I seem to attract them. Please, sit and join us for breakfast."

"I have already eaten," replied Stopus, "but I'll join you with coffee. I do enjoy a good mug of coffee." Stopus sat down and popped a grape into his mouth with a grin.

"Alright, then." Joneya took another bite of toast and then held her coffee mug against her lower lip. "So what do we know this morning that we didn't know before?"

"I knew before that you lissten, but I am glad to ssee that you thought about what I ssaid and reached for your genuine power."

"My what?" Joneya looked momentarily confused. "Oh."

"Oh, indeed. I am glad that you found your way to partner with King sssCern for more than ceremoniesss."

Cern said nothing, but raised an eyebrow.

"He did plant the seed that perhaps I am not using the wealth of power and knowledge that I have available," Joneya admitted.

"Perhapsss?" Stopus' turn to lift an eyebrow.

"I do use it sometimes, but certainly not as much as I could. Agreed?"

"Almosst." Stopus smiled again. "You are more aware now and will move into your full power if you continue. I agree that you opened your eyesss."

Cern spoke up then, "We seem to be partners here. At least for now. So yes, I have spread my dryads and nymphs through the realms to gather the whispers on the wind and in the streams. The trees are already reporting back."

"Good. I think perhapss we need to focusss on the vampyresss. I understand they are being, ahhh, what isss the word? Ahh, courierss, yesss, that'sss it."

"Couriers-?"

"Vampires-?"

Joneya and Cern spoke at once, looked at each other, and then looked back to Stopus. Clearly, he would need to answer both questions.

Stopus smiled without mirth. "Yesss, vampyre couriersss. But they do not carry messagesss, but insstead small packagesss."

Joneya held her silence and waited for more. Cern followed her lead, but laid a firm hand on her thigh, sending calming energy between them.

Cern's hand on her leg was like a white hot flame and then a conduit as warmth and strength coursed through her like the wind before a storm. Just then, laughing children came tumbling into the dining room, cutting short all adult conversations.

Larseth led a couple of older boys to the buffet table for bacon, Ravenous just a step behind. A group of giggling girls with Arigail in the lead and Elfrya in the midst came over and said a hurried good morning to Joneya and then fell on the fruit and muffins. Cantaloupe was Elfrya's favorite and she took several pieces and a tall glass of milk. Arigail always chose more than she actually ate, but today her friends would help clean her plate of the sweets and the berries while she sipped her Sleepytime® tea. The boys devoured pastries and bacon while gulping down glasses of juice. There was a momentary lull while all the children's mouths were full, but that soon ended in a fit of giggles.

Laughing, Joneya said to Cern and Stopus, "I would suggest we move to the library to continue this conversation of messengers and ghouls, but I think this gaggle of noise is inhaling their food and sure to leave before long."

Cern grinned his agreement, and Stopus merely inclined his head to her. The hilarity lasted a few minutes longer as the children worked out plans to visit the barns and to a giant game of tag in the large backyard. Joneya missed the last of their planning when Declan came over and whispered in her ear.

"There's a visitor to see you, M'Lady. She said she would wait by your study door. I suggested that it was damp there in the shade and she wait in the hall, but she refused." Sir Ned was already moving, but Joneya knew who it was.

"Trust me, Declan, she doesn't mind the damp." Joneya bit her lip a moment, eyes roving over the gaggle of children. "Alright, Kiddos, you're headed to the barns now, while the grass dries?"

"Well-"

"It's hard to play tag in slippery grass, nor can you play hide n seek if your footprints lead the way." The older children quickly realized that she was right and hurriedly grabbed their seconds, or thirds, of favorite foods to finish their rowdy breakfast. "Declan," Joneya continued, "please offer the woman a glass of water from the red covered carafe on my table, but swirl it around to remix the flavorings first. Tell her that we'll be there as soon as I have the children settled."

Declan looked puzzled as no one ever used the red carafe but left with haste to do as his queen asked.

It was a tense group in Joneya's study as Cern, Sir Ned, Stopus, the woman, and Joneya sat around the table. Declan brought fresh coffee for the group and an enormous glass of water for the mystery woman. As soon as he left, Joneya stood and reached forward to take the glass. "Sorry, he doesn't know." She tipped the glass into several of the plants around the room and then returned to fill the glass from the red carafe and gently set both down on the table.

"More sstrange friendsss, you keep, my queen."

"Yeah." Joneya had only just risen, but she was already tired. Tired of figuring out a puzzle, tired of juggling roles, and tired of always being the center pin of the lock. "So it seems." She pointedly looked at Stopus.

"Touche."

"I'm sure we all know each other by reputation, but let's introduce ourselves, yeah?" Joneya asked, but wasn't really asking. It was obvious that they all knew of each other's kinds, but that didn't actually mean that they knew of each other. It was a gracious way to lead them to familiarity.

"Welcome to my home, House Isilme. I've been away a long time, but my family and I have returned now. Apparently, not everyone is happy to see us, since my husband, Abaris, cannot join us at this meeting."

Stopus snorted, "Indeed, my queen, that was a grasciousss way to put it." Joneya smiled and tipped her head at him. "I am Ssstopusss. You might guesss that I am not from around here. I come from another realm, and lead my family and the guivre. I felt the dissturbancsess and heard ssome rumorss, sso I am here."

Sir Ned nodded at Stopus and looked round the table making eye contact with each of them. "I have met with all of you, so I don't think you need much from me. I'm Ned, Fist of the Blood."

The woman held only Joneya's gaze as she spoke in her rusty, gravelly voice, "I am Muirgen. I speak for the Merfolk here." Joneya gave a nod of a salute to the woman who seldom shared her name and to do so now, spoke volumes of the importance of the moment and the strength of their friendship.

Cern had shifted when Muirgen spoke. He looked at her with admiration and nodded respectfully. "My Lady." Then he shifted his eyes around the table. "I am Cern. I have several roles in the realm, but I am best known for being the Stag King. I am the voice of the nature spirits."

"Welcome all." As she spoke, Joneya raised her mug in a toast. Everyone around the table raised their mugs and glasses, then clanked their vessels together with the age old tradition of slopping the beverages together, assuring their mutual safety. "Stopus, you were about to explain something about couriers-"

"-and vampires," added Cern.

"-and vampires," smiled Joneya "when we were so thoroughly interrupted by children."

"Yesss, I wass," agreed Stopus with an indulgent smile. "Firsst, you do know the difference between vampiresss and vampyresss, yesss?"

Glancing quickly around the table, Joneya answered, "Yes, in that we understand the former to be like any other species, a mix of good and bad members. The latter, however, are bloodthirsty and conniving. The Vampires also often coexist with humans, just with extra caution around some situations."

"Yesss. Often the vampyres are said to be greedy and evil. There are exceptionsss of courssse, but overwhelmingly they are...not nice."

"And, pardon me for asking you to repeat yourself, but which did you say: vampires or vampyres?" asked Cern.

"We must be clear," added Muirgen.

"Indeed, we musst be very clear," Stopus agreed. "It is the vampyresss that bear invesstigation right now. I know that they are couriering packages of some sort between this world and another. They are being notissed asss they are ruthlessss enough to always receive their paymentsss or their packagesss."

Sir Ned was nodding. "Couriers fits with the blackmailing and the sudden increase in debts being an issue."

"Indeed," said Stopus.

"Ok, but whom are they trading? Where are the packages going and coming from? Or is it even the same place?"

"Apparently, we need to arrange to buy something," mused Joneya.

"It might help, my queen, if we knew just what it was we want to buy," said Cern with a dark chuckle.

"If it's illegal, it's either drugs, sex, or similar," suggested Sir Ned.

"Uhhuh."

"I think," rasped Muirgen, "that it is drugs. We have had an increase in overdoses over the past six months or so. It ties along to so many of my people upset and injured over their waters being raped by new speedboats and pollution."

"What new speedboats?" asked Joneya, with wide eyes.

"I was going to speak to you, Joneya. Our safe waters, those that have been banned from the fishing fleets and larger ships, have been interrupted more and more by speeding boats cutting through at high speeds. It is no longer safe for our children to grow, learn, and play in their nursery waters."

"That's not ok!" Joneya was angry. "Those are sacred waters and no one other than sea creatures are supposed to be there except the occasional storm nymphs."

"That was the agreement, yes." Muirgen's nostrils flared and her eyes flashed. "We thought you were aware."

"How could I possibly know this? I prohibit the navy from looking there or traveling there to keep your secrets safe."

"Easy, my ladies." Sir Ned made soothing gestures with his hands. "We'll sort this out. With your permission, Muirgen, I will assign some men I trust to keep watch on your boundaries, not entering in, to see these boats that are cutting through. Perhaps you could arrange to deliver some of the trash that they are dropping. There may be clues we can use."

Muirgen took a deep breath, followed by a long swallow of her water. "Yes, I'm sorry for my attitude. We would appreciate your help.

And if you find a pattern so you think entering is the only way to catch these interlopers, then we shall have to find a way to work together."

"Yes, ma'am, but we'll try to avoid your waters as much as possible." Sir Ned rubbed his nose as he chose his words carefully, "In exchange, Muirgen, would you be able to, ah, to persuade your people to not-"

Muirgen laughed huskily and interrupted, "Yes, Sir Ned. We will alleviate our siren's song near your crews as they work to help us. I cannot guarantee that my sisters will not tease your crews, but I will guide them to not harm your crews or cause them to harm themselves."

Sir Ned nodded his head in understanding and agreement. "I appreciate that."

\*\*\*

The morning moved on as they discussed how to best deal with this Trouble. It did seem logical that all three of the Big Troubles seemed to be related: drugs, debts/blackmail, and Abaris' kidnapping. Ending any one of the Troubles would affect the other, but what course of action would solve all three? It would be better to go slowly and eradicate all three problems than stop one and send the other two deeper underground.

"We all agree that we stop the naval ships that are probably transporting drugs. And we need to do that asap," Joneya said what they all knew to be true. "However, we need a plan today of what else to do to stop this. I won't wait to save the Merwaters, so how do we hit this drug operation?"

"Do we have someone who can look like they need a fast source of cash and become a courier or whatever on this side?" Sir Ned thought aloud.

"My queen, you can put out an announcement that there were erroneous loans given out and now you are calling those debts in," suggested Cern. "It might stress a few innocent people a bit, but it offers an excuse for a wide number of people suddenly needing cash."

Joneya looked unconvinced.

"He isss right," agreed Stopus. "You can also offer that you will deduct a persssentage if they can repay it within three monthsss. Thisss givesss a reason for everyone to be in a hurry. But it alssso can alleviate sstressss for the innosssent asss you can alsso offer a payment plan for anyone who needsss it. Only we know that it isss all bogusss."

"It could work," offered Sir Ned.

"Hmmm," Joneya chewed the inside of her lip. "So we provide an excuse for an unknown number of people to suddenly need money. While giving an out to the rest of the people who don't actually exist, so that worrywarts won't worry as much. I don't exactly like it, but I don't have anything better."

"We need to find who can be our little spies without stirring attention. My people don't exactly fit in..." suggested Cern.

"I may have a couple of people who can be undercover," mused Sir Ned.

"No!" said Stopus emphatically. "Your copsss will alwaysss be copsss."

"They do have a bit of a stiff feel," agreed Cern with a smile.

"Do we find a loyal villager?" asked Joneya.

"We don't have to infiltrate from this side, maybe. Maybe we do it from the other side?"

"Really? Do you know someone over there?"

"Or where that is exactly?"

"Well, I um, hmm."

# Chapter 13 - Operation Seascapes

We all have that voice inside us that says, "Get up, Get UP! You can never beat us because we'll always get back up. We're too stubborn to just give up, right?" He looked sincere and worn enough to be someone decent enough who was just on hard times.

The tall, dark-haired, brooding man nodded his head over to the other lanky, platinum blond man. Both looked like they worked in an office all day - no tan, perfectly dressed and manicured. They conferred quickly, and then the blond man nodded and walked a bit away. The dark-haired man returned.

"Yeah, ok. We'll try you, but no funny business, yeah? If I even think you're crossing us, or turning canary, your mama will never see you again. Straight?"

"Yeah. I get it." He looked a little miserable. "I don't want no trouble. I just need some cash. Just a little."

"How much is a little?"

"Enough," he could see avoiding it wasn't going to work. "About a $100,000," he mumbled.

The dark-haired man let out a whistle, "Yeah, ok I see your incentive. I think you understand ours. So, we can work together. And maybe, when you see how easy this is, maybe you want to stay for a little more than just the money you seem to owe."

"Yeah, we'll see."

"Alright, get a burner phone. I'll give you one now, but you replace it every week. There is one number programmed in it. You don't ever call that number. But it will text you and set up meeting spots. You go where it tells you, when it tells you. When you get there, you get more information. Most likely the person who meets you won't have any more information than you, just a package and an address for you. Got it?"

"I think so."

***

On a different phone, damn, he had three damn phones now. Only the cases told them apart. "Yeah, I'm in. They're cautious, though. ... Yeah, I'll do this pass with just the burner phone and nothing else. They don't have any reason to trust me yet. ... yeah. Ok."

***

Mr. Platinum Blond, also known as Pavlo Schmirt, stood very still and scanned him as he came through the gate. By standing just behind it, he could clearly see the nervous young man, but couldn't be seen unless the young man moved around and then behind the gate. Pavlo saw him step through and shiver slightly. Apparently he could feel gates, good. Better, he didn't carry any odd electrical energies like if he had an extra device, or batteries, or a tracking device on him. He might have a hidden ward webbing him to another magic wielder, but otherwise, he seemed clean. And nervous. He seemed very nervous, not surprising. The quick background check that Pavlo had done showed him to be a graduate student of history who bartended in his spare time, and had been seen coming out of gambling houses of late. His spending had been quite high a year or so ago, but not recently. Indeed, the pizza delivery driver that Pavlo had questioned said that this guy had been one of his best tippers until a week or so ago.

Pavlo watched the young man spot the assigned bench and, after glancing around, walked over and pulled out his book. Just like he was supposed to do, if it was a decent day. There was a back-up plan for rainy days, but it just wasn't as slick. He still had hunched shoulders and dropped his book once, but overall he seemed to be doing alright. Soon, a tall, svelte woman in black leather boots, a very short skirt, black blouse, and platinum a ponytail pulled up high, sat down beside him. She rubbed her ankle a little and then took off her boot, setting it on the bench between them. As she rubbed her ankle and foot, Pavlo could see her lips move and the young man jump.

Clearly following her instructions very carefully, he eased a small black pouch out of her boot and slid it into his pocket while pretending to continue reading. Then, Miss Platinum Ponytail said something a little louder, and the young man laughed. It sounded a little forced, but no more than nerves might account for with a beautiful girl suddenly sitting beside you.

She laughed again and then slid her boot back on. The young man gave a genuine-looking grin and laughed again, too. She stood up, gave a little bow, and spun so fast that her ponytail whirled out straight and she continued walking along. She passed right past Pavlo. She winked at him and hissed as she passed, "He might be so nervous that he pissed himself, but he also follows directions."

Pavlo nodded to her and kept watching the young man. Nervously the young man checked his watch and then slouched back down on the bench, trying to read, and every once in a while patting his pocket as if it might have mysteriously opened and dropped the contents. After about five minutes, the young man checked his watch again. He gave a large stretch and yawned. He sat another moment, looking around the park as if actually admiring the view. He tipped his head back and let the sun warm his face for a moment. He stood up, looked around again and then loped off at a quick pace the way he had come, through the gate and disappearing without ever seeing Pavlo.

"Oh my god, it is so hard to pretend to be nervous, when you are so confident in a plan working!" laughed a young man spinning a little back and forth on a bar stool. He was still amped up.

"Oh yeah? Try sailing through waters your mam told you never ta go fore she knew the sirens had taken yer auld grandad from there." He gulped some more beer from the frosty mug. "I can't explain how unnaturally still those waters were. We were definitely being watched by…something."

"Like what?"

"No, like a who. Well, dangerous enough to be a what, but definitely a who."

"What?!"

"Yeah. I dunno. It just felt…wrong."

"Why were you even there? I thought those waters were off limits?"

"Yeah, some special assignment for people sailing through and possibly dumping stuff. But what about you? You were undercover?!"

"Yut, some sort of drug deal, trying to find out who the higher-ups are, not just the street sellers. I'm s'posed to be some schmuck looking to earn some fast cash."

"Oh yeah, that makes sense."

"I'm not some poor scared schmuck though, so I had to pretend to be nervous and it was hard. But there was this hot chick -I mean damn, she was something. Tall and curvy and blond, blond hair. I could entertain her for hours, if you know what I mean."

The men continued their bar talk until late in the evening over beer. It was probably a good thing that the "hot chick" never heard their ideas of entertainment with her or any other available woman, or they might both have been eviscerated and turned into eunuchs.

*** 

Joneya's council met regularly to receive updates, and it did not take long for the undercover gentleman to be regularly transporting "goods" and money transactions through the gates. The blond woman was the usual contact, but sometimes it was some other nervous person who handed off an envelope or package.

Tuesday afternoon, they were meeting in the shade outside in a pavilion. Cern was speaking softly, "I understand there was something different about the meeting yesterday?"

Sir Ned answered, "Indeed. Until now, all the transactions have been calm and productive. However, yesterday, our undercover courier could not pick up the scheduled envelope. Therefore, he had to travel to the bench meeting without it."

"Bench meeting?"

"Sorry, that's what we have started calling it since they always meet at the bench." Seeing the looks of understanding, Sir Ned continued, "We were concerned that there might be a consequence for our young undercover, but actually the blond woman seemed quite calm. She made our agent repeat his story several times with exactly what happened, but I think that was more to check his honesty, that he didn't steal the cash. Anyway, she said she would handle the next step and that he needn't collect from that person anymore until he heard otherwise.

"You may remember," Sir Ned clarified, "that our agent had started having a few regular stops and was picking up the same type of envelope every day from the same people at the same time. This was one of those, so we assume it is important that she instructed him to desist."

Cern mused, "We should watch to see if there is an unfortunate incident that befalls this person. I mean to say, the person who was supposed to supply the envelope. I would be interested in knowing how they handle someone not paying their debt."

"Indeed," Joneya mused. "Cern, do you have any nymphs in that vicinity that could hide in a tree or such? I don't think someone could hide for long in a car without being observed, and there is no way to arrange an apartment opposite to watch from in this short time frame."

"Of course. I'll arrange it."

"What do we think might happen?"

"I'm not sure, but instruct your nymph not to be involved in anything that might hurt her. Her safety is more important."

"Agreed, but she is good at hiding in the branches of the trees. She will be fine."

Sir Ned spoke up and said, "We do need to be aware that these people have been known to have a swift and sometimes brutal way of handling business. I suggest we give our agent a few extra days' break in-between his assignments, just to be on the safe side."

Cern nodded in agreement and said, "If something does happen to the supplier, it might help us piece together some clues as to who the higher-ups are in this organization. We haven't been able to get very far up this particular chain of command."

Joneya thought for a moment and said, "In that case, perhaps it's worthwhile for the nymph to get a closer look. She won't arouse suspicion if she's blending in with the trees and watching the activity. She did well in her last task."

"My men are now accustomed to receiving notes deposited by squirrels. Who knew rodents could be good messengers?" Sir Ned worked hard to suppress his smile.

The small group discussed the risks and the potential reward for such an endeavor. After a lengthy debate, they agreed to the plan.

Joneya said, "We should monitor the situation carefully and be prepared to respond to any suspicious activity. I'm sure our agent can help us if needed."

The group nodded in agreement, and with that, the conversation came to a close. Now it was just a waiting game. They would have to wait and see if anything happened to the supplier— and what it might mean for their mission.

***

"But I'm so worried." Her words were soft, but Cern knew the angst that they carried as Joneya spoke.

"He's strong."

"Not for this. He wasn't born into this. He has no idea what's going on. I never really explained any of these powers to him and I certainly never explained my heritage, my blood, this history. He was completely unprepared!"

"Not completely." Cern stayed calm and spoke reasonably. He knew his queen was upset, but she was still the people's true queen. She was queen of the land, too, and they didn't need a tempest stirring up because her emotions were in upheaval. "You have spoken of him as a hunter. He must have instincts then, and the ability to observe and listen."

Joneya chewed the inside of her lip, considering. "True. In normal situations, he can care for himself. In almost any situation of danger, in fact. But this is deeper and magic is not something he knows. If they have glamored anything or tease his senses, he may not even know that they are fucking with him-" She took a deep breath.

Joneya knew that Abaris was capable. She also knew that her enemies would stop at nearly nothing to destroy her or try to steal her power. Her greatest fear was that ultimately she would be forced to choose between the land and her people over her family. The Old Blood was in her children too, but that would be the only reason to justify their lives over anything magical to protect the land. It would destroy her to sacrifice her family to save the land or to sacrifice her people to save her family. In that very way, she might destroy exactly what she meant to save. It couldn't come to that.

"Easy, Love. Breathe."

"I know." Joneya took a calming breath and cracked her neck from side to side.

Cern came behind her, and his strong fingers worked her neck and shoulders. His strength slid into her, magic singing to magic. A breeze entered the window, salty sea air mixed with new meadow grass and a hint of autumn leaves.

"Yeah. Rub a little more please, so my headache eases." Joneya cracked her neck again and stretched it forward as Cern worked his fingers against the knotted muscles. "I don't have to choose. We'll find him and bring him home, but no matter what, we protect my children above and beyond me."

"Not beyond-"

"Yes, if there must be a choice, they are saved. One or both of them will take my place someday. They both can read the runes."

Cern's intake of breath was echoed by Sir Ned in the doorway.

"You're sure?" asked Sir Ned in his quiet, serious voice.

"Absolutely."

"Two," breathed Sir Ned.

"And they're not even twins," echoed Cern in wonder.

***

End of Book One of Through The Gate. Look for book two in the fall of 2024.

# Author's note:

I very much hope you enjoyed this story! In which case, a review would mean the world to me - indie authors desperately need reviews of 4* or more for the bigger platforms to even show our books.

If you enjoyed this story, you might also enjoy (with Arichel and her court). You can find all of my stories here on my Linktree: . I would love for you to join my reader groups on Facebook and/or join my early access on Ream! Never forget authors love to hear from you, too, so please reach out by email or social media.

Thank you for your support and have a wonderful day!

Rachel Roy